FRENCH QUARTER FAE

TWISTED SISTERS MIDLIFE MAELSTROM BOOK #4

BRENDA TRIM

Copyright © November 2022 by Brenda Trim
Editor: Chris Cain & Kelly Smyczynski
Cover Art by Fiona Jayde

* * *

This book is a work of fiction. The names, characters, places, and incidents are products of the writers' imagination or have been used fictitiously and are not to be construed as real. Any resemblance to persons, living or dead, actual events, locales or organizations is entirely coincidental.

WARNING: The unauthorized reproduction of this work is illegal. Criminal copyright infringement is investigated by the FBI and is punishable by up to 5 years in federal prison and a fine of $250,000.

All rights reserved. With the exception of quotes used in reviews, this book may not be reproduced or used in whole or in part by any means existing without written permission from the authors.

❦ Created with Vellum

Sisters don't need words - we've already got our own language of eye rolls, winks, laughs, sighs, and screams.

CHAPTER 1

DAHLIA

I moaned as the garlic, basil, and cheese burst over my taste buds. "That is so freaking delicious. I need the recipe for this pizza dough. Mine always tastes more like bread. It needs to be chewier, like this."

Lucas lifted his hand to get the attention of the waiter. "Can you bring Chef Daniels out here, please? Tell him Lucas is here to talk to him."

My mouth parted in surprise. I learned something new about Lucas every day. It was slightly disturbing to think of his commitment to me despite how little we actually knew of one another. I was adjusting to the magical world rapidly, but my mind still operated like a mundie in some fundamental ways.

Cocking my head to the side I smirked at him. "Do you know people everywhere? I thought this was a mundie owned business."

Lucas set his piece of pizza down and wiped his mouth. "I've been alive longer than you, Flower."

The reminder of our age differences used to make me uncomfortable. I was in my mid-forties while he was in his mid-seventies. For mundies that would have been a major difference. Lucas was a shifter and they lived long lives and aged at a slower rate than humans. No one knew how my sisters and I would age from here on because we were magical mutts.

A few short months ago we were normal mundies that had purchased a rundown plantation together. We changed completely when a powerful witch visited us at Willowberry and lifted a curse on our property, unlocking our dormant magical DNA in the process.

"You don't have to try and impress me with your connections. Having your pack help me fight zombies did that." I smiled at him as I took another bite.

A handsome guy with close cropped, brown hair approached our table right then. He clapped Lucas's extended hand. "Hey, Luc. How's it going?"

"It's great, Nigel. I'd like to introduce my mate, Dahlia. She and her five sisters own the Willowberry Plantation." Lucas gestured to me as I tried my best to chew fast and swallow my food.

My cheeks heated as I dipped my head and forced the cheesy dough down my gullet. It got stuck making my choke and start coughing. Lucas handed me my water and patted my back, asking if I was alright. It took a couple of seconds before I managed to get the wad of crust down past my esophagus so I could breathe and speak again.

Nodding, I shook the hand Nigel had been holding out to me. "Sorry. That went down the wrong pipe."

Nigel smiled revealing even white teeth. "It's alright. Luc caught you mid-bite. I've heard of the fabulous events you and your sisters throw. How did this riffraff land such a gem as yourself?"

I chuckled and landed a hand over Lucas's on the table. "I'm the one that got lucky."

Lucas turned his hand over and twined our fingers together. "Fate brought us together."

"The way I hear it, she also brought the sisters into our world to turn it on its head," Nigel added.

My gaze traveled over Nigel's face from his blue eyes to his slightly crooked nose and big smile. He was magazine worthy, but nothing told me what kind of paranormal creature he was.

Lucas leaned toward me. "He's a mage."

"Ah," I said as I looked up at Nigel. "I'm still getting used to everything in this world, so you'll have to excuse me."

Nigel tilted his head from side to side. "It's understandable. It's a major change from what you were used to and there are so many nuances and things to consider. Although, from what I hear, you and your sisters are making your own rules."

My back straightened and a smile swept over my face. I'd always marched to my own drummer. Especially when it meant trampling injustice. It was one reason I went into social work to begin with, "We think of it as redefining guidelines. No one individual should have absolute power over others. Just because something has been done a certain way doesn't mean it should stay that way."

Lucas beamed with pride. "Your integrity is one reason so many are supporting your changes. They know you aren't trying to step in and take power for yourselves."

"Lucas is right. What you and your sisters have stirred up has given other leaders the courage to take action of their own," Nigel added.

The thought that we sparked something by freeing the

necromancers from Marie Leveau's control was thrilling. Change was good. And from what I'd seen the magical world in New Orleans needed it. "That's encouraging. We'd hate to do all of this and have her force everyone back in line."

"I can't see that happening. Anyway, is there anything I can do for you before I go back to the kitchen?" I welcomed Nigel's change of subject. The last thing I wanted to do during my date with Lucas was get involved in a political debate.

Lucas nodded as he let go of my hand and picked up his slice. "Lia and I were just talking about how you get your dough to the perfect consistency."

My cheeks were pink but I wasn't going to turn away any advice. "It's nice and chewy which is something I can never manage."

Nigel chuckled as he waved his hands in front of him. "You should start with using a long rise time before you knead, knead, knead it. It also helps to use a recipe with more salt, as well. Honestly, I credit the flavor and consistency of mine to the starter that I use. It's been in my family for seventy years."

A gasp escaped my mouth. "I'll try your tips but I'm not going to count on it being different. That starter is no doubt one key to your success. My former mother-in-law used to have a sourdough starter she got from her grandmother, and it made the best bread I've ever eaten."

"If you're familiar with using a starter I'm happy to share some of mine with you," Nigel offered. "Although, I shouldn't. It'd be bad for business." He winked at me making Lucas scowl at his friend.

"I'll take it because my sister Dakota will be able to work wonders with it. I'm not actually familiar with using starters. I enjoy cooking, but never had have much time to perfect my skills," I admitted. There was no need to tell him I didn't inherit the starter from Leo's mom. She didn't even speak to me anymore.

Nigel inclined his head as something near the kitchen caught his eye. "I'll have some brought out to you. It was nice meeting you, Dahlia. I look forward to seeing you again."

I held up a hand. "I'd like that. In fact, I know you don't offer catering but I would love to talk to you about doing special events at Willowberry. My brother-in-law put in a stone pizza oven when we renovated."

Nigel's eyes lit up. "That's an intriguing offer. I've wanted to expand. Lucas has my number. Let's chat soon."

Lucas and I thanked the chef before he took off to the kitchen at a rapid pace. Lucas lifted my hand and kissed the back of it. "Are you ready to head home? I have more planned for you this evening."

My mind raced with naughty thoughts as I wiped my mouth and dropped my napkin on my plate. "I like the way you think, Chief."

Lucas wrinkled his nose as he signaled the waiter again. "I'm not sure I like that nickname," he told me before focusing on the server. "Can we get a couple of boxes and the check, please."

I smiled sweetly at Lucas as the waiter left to do as asked. "You're stuck with it now. You shouldn't be such a dominating man and I'd have come up with something else. Perhaps you'd like stud muffin better."

Lucas chuckled as he shook his head. "Chief it is, then."

Lucas paid the bill and accepted the boxes and container of dough from the server. We were out the door and headed across the French Quarter to the lot where Lucas had parked his truck, when my arms prickled with an unfamiliar energy. I scanned our surroundings searching for the source of my discomfort. Everything looked like it should. The restaurants and bars were crowded with patrons. The mundies laughed and joked with one another with drinks in their hands. The moon and stars above were bright and the heat of a summer night caused a light sheen of sweat to cover my body.

Of course, that could have been caused by one of those 'heat things' as Deandra called them. At forty years old, Dea had only experienced a couple of them, so she wasn't truly familiar with how awful hot flashes could be.

Unable to banish the sensation that something was wrong, I tugged on Lucas's hand. "Do you feel that?"

Lucas lifted the bag in his hand and gestured to a darkened courtyard in front of us. "If I'm not mistaken there's a vampire up ahead."

I moved closer to his side as I recalled the one encounter Dani and I'd had with a couple of vamps at Brezok's bar a while back. They'd tried to put us under a thrall with the intention of making us compliant so they could feed from us. But they'd still overpowered us and without Nedesea's help we would not have gotten away unharmed. That was after Phoebe told us how vampires in my city had nearly killed Stella. None of that made me like them much.

I was so focused on the area where Lucas believed the vampire was hiding that I missed the monster loping across Jackson Square. Lucas shoved the bag into my hand and shifted his hands into claws at the same time people started screaming. I opened my purse hoping to find a weapon but came up empty. Instead, I grabbed my phone and asked Siri to text Kaitlyn about sending someone to my location to deal with mundies before they got away. I could see numerous cell phones come out with their cameras aimed at the sight of Lucas charging a creature that looked like a cross between a bear and a dog. It's orange eyes and sharp claws had me shaking as my boyfriend rammed into the thing. The beast tossed Lucas over its head making him crash into a group of mundies that were recording the showdown.

Getting a clear picture was easy thanks to Hollywood and the countless shows I'd seen where thieves or spies disabled alarms with a device that did something similar. I took a moment to concentrate my intent creating an electromagnetic pulse that would disable the electronics in the area. I needed to keep my new world safe. With my intent clear in my mind, I chanted, *"Electro pulsum."* Energy rushed out of me as soon as the words left my mouth. The force of it made me stumble forward. My movement caught the monster's attention and it headed right for me.

Ignoring the mundies cursing about their cell phones not working, I ran toward the park a few feet away. There were fewer mundies to get hurt there, conjuring the amber flames of my witch fire as I went. I considered trying to shift my hands into dragon talons, but that still took too much effort for me.

Claws scraped across my back and I fell to my knees, abrading the shit out of them, as I hit the sidewalk. Curses flew from my mouth as I lost the bag with the pizza dough starter and our leftovers. I was really looking forward to trying my hand at dough with Dakota.

Lucas was there before the monster managed to get in another blow. I watched his fist slam into the side of the bear-dog's head. As a shifter and the alpha of his pack, Lucas was strong as hell, yet his punch didn't faze the beast.

Lucas wrapped an arm around the creature's neck and yanked it away from me. I called up my fire again and pressed my palms to the monster's legs. It ignited the fur covering its limbs instantly. I willed the flames to burn through flesh and muscle but not travel and hurt Lucas. I couldn't let it go completely or Lucas would get hurt.

I kicked the monster making it drop to its knees. Lucas

sliced open the side of its neck making blood gush out of the wound. People started screaming then. I imagined the mundies assumed we were filming a movie or something because New Orleans was a popular location for movie and television production.

"*Nolite movere,*" I blurted the second the thought entered my mind. I didn't have time to firm up my intent. My mind whirled as I watched Lucas handle the monster, wondering where it came from. It had a dark green aura with black lines running throughout. I coaxed my flames to spread over the monster when Lucas lifted his touch from the thing. The scent of burning fur and flesh turned my stomach.

"Lia," Kaitlyn cried out.

My head snapped in her direction, and I winced when the movement made the cut along my upper back pull open. "Thank God, you're here. I have no idea where this thing came from. It just started attacking. I fried the phones and stopped the mundies from leaving. I didn't want to try and erase their memories. I was afraid I'd fry their brains instead." The words came out in rapid fire when the head witch stopped in front of me.

Kaitlyn turned me gently with a hand on my shoulder. I felt heat emanate from her hand and seep into the wound. I realized she stopped the bleeding when the warm trickle ebbed. "You did good. I'm glad you didn't try to erase anyone's memories. All you would have done was turn their brains to mush. We leave that to vampires. Anton is on his way here to help deal with this mess."

I couldn't relax with her assurances, but I did bend and pick up the bag I'd dropped, hoping the dough and left overs were still good inside. Lucas kicked the creature and I extinguished my fire. "What is that? And why would it attack in the French Quarter?"

Kaitlyn covered her nose as she bent closer to the thing. I

couldn't imagine closing the distance to it. It smelled bad enough from several feet away. "I didn't get a good look at it before your flames burned it. What did it look like?" Kaitlyn asked.

I recounted what I'd seen to Kaitlyn at the same time Lucas's eyes narrowed on a guy heading in our direction from Decatur. It looked like he was coming from the river on the other side of that street.

"It sounds like a barghest. It's a Fae creature," Kaitlyn said then followed my gaze when she noticed I wasn't paying attention. The head witch lifted a hand. "Thank you for coming Anton. As you can see, we need your assistance erasing the last half an hour from the minds of the mundies that witnessed this incident."

Anton inclined his head then settled his stormy gray eyes on me. "I'd be happy to help, but only because I assume you aren't the ones that brought this beast from the Fae realm."

Lucas snarled at the vampire. "We all have to work together to protect our identities. Your kind would be hunted first. And no, we didn't bring it here."

Kaitlyn lifted her hands and gestured around them. "Lucas is right, we have to cooperate with each other. Anton came when I asked, Lucas. He's here to help. Now, what matters is keeping the magical world a secret. Dahlia and I will get answers as to how this happened."

My heart was racing as I watched the vampire incline his blond head to Kaitlyn before he faced the shadowed courtyard Lucas had pointed out earlier and whistled. Several men and women emerged from the shadows and started moving through the mundies still frozen by my spell.

"How are we supposed to find out how this barghest got here?" I asked Kaitlyn, deciding to focus on the problem I could maybe do something about.

Kaitlyn pursed her lips. "We need to talk to Fae and elves

that live in the area. I can't imagine any of them traveling to Cottlehill in England and asking for permission to retrieve a barghest. The portal guardians wouldn't allow it even if they had."

My head was pounding, and I was afraid the mixture of smells would trigger my smell-o-vision and make me see something. It was a miracle I hadn't had a premonition yet.

I ran a hand down my face. "Send me a list of Fae. Lucas and I will go ask some questions."

Kaitlyn clapped a hand on my shoulder. "I'll pay a visit to my friends and see if they heard anything. You go home and rest. Anton and his people have the mundies handled. Everything else can wait."

My shoulder sagged and I threw my arms around her neck. "Perfect. Thank you."

Kaitlyn nodded and then headed over to Anton. I watched Kaitlyn leave with the vampire right behind her before turning to Lucas. "Why is it that our dates always seem to be interrupted by an angry god or a monster?"

Lucas sighed and brushed my hair away from my face. "I think dark beings are drawn to your light, Flower. It frightens them and makes them want to extinguish it before it burns them to ash."

I snorted as I started walking. "I had no idea I was some kind of lighthouse. I'll have to find a way to dim my beacon, so we can get some peace."

Lucas tugged me into his arms and pressed his lips to mine for a brief, yet passionate kiss. "You keep me on my toes. Don't ever try to stifle anything about yourself. I love you no matter what comes our way."

My heart raced as every cell in my body warmed from his affection. I hadn't dreamed of having a partner like Lucas. My first husband, Leo wasn't perfect. In many ways, he tried to make me conform to what he preferred. Lucas was the first to accept me as I was and wanted to keep me that way.

"Good because we need to find out what's going on with the Fae in the French Quarter." Experience told me that the attack by the Fae monster was just the beginning. If Marie was behind this latest monster, things were about to get ugly, fast.

CHAPTER 2

DANIELLE

I gaped at Lia as she draped the dark grey tablecloth over the clothes line to dry. Typically, we dry cleaned them, but we were offering wine and cheeses for what Phi had termed a ghost tour of the plantation. Delphine figured that with the fascination for the paranormal, we could offer an early evening tour for adults once a month where Cami told stories of the matron haunting the halls. Mundies would have no idea that Cami's stories were detailed and vivid because she was alive when the house was built.

Cami had given us a dry run through what she planned on telling guests and, in the process, gave us a new appreciation for what she had lived through. We'd known her life had been traumatic, as was her death. It was easy to forget because she was here with us now and rarely talked about her past. My heart broke for her because I had the memories to go with her stories thanks to my psychometric power.

FRENCH QUARTER FAE

Those abilities were also why I had taken to wearing gloves in my own home.

When my sisters and I discovered we had magical powers, I was excited to be part of the magical world. That faded fast with the weight of seeing so much suffering. Of course, it wasn't all bad. However, it was difficult to put the bad out of my head to focus on the good.

Shaking my head, I tugged the fabric and straightened it so it would dry while refocusing on the events Dahlia had shared with me. "Why am I not surprised your date was interrupted by some crazed monster? Why is this our problem? Let Kaitlyn and the others handle it." I didn't mind tackling the various problems that had come up for us, but I wasn't as eager for the Twisted Sisters to become the magical detectives in New Orleans, like Lia and Kota seemed to be.

My priority was on expanding the Six Twisted Sisters event planning business and venue. We handled various parties and celebrations for the mundie and magical worlds. The Willowberry Plantation was our baby. The six of us had put everything we had into the place. Lia and I had even sold our homes and lived in the place. I was happier putting my efforts into our property than chasing deranged loa, ghosts, and zombies. Not to mention all we seemed to do was piss off the Queen of Voodoo. Admittedly, that was highly satisfying. And I did like being a vehicle for change.

It was nice to be part of getting people, like Temperence, free from Marie Leveau's oppressive control. She'd forced the necromancers to do her bidding and had gone unchecked for far too long. I believed she was a major reason there were so many problems at the moment. Alright, so I enjoyed being part of these situations more than I wanted to admit. *You don't like not being a highly skilled witch.* I hated when my mind pointed out the truth. There were times I preferred to stay in the dark.

Lia sighed as she picked up the basket and headed back to the main house. "I know you don't like getting involved in shit and you don't have to, but I can't ignore it. Like usual, I was dragged into the middle of it. We can discuss that later though. Right now, we need to make sure we're prepared to show Stasia her options."

The tension in my shoulders relaxed when Lia refocused on something that was right up my alley. Creating the perfect event for someone made my heart happy and I was good at it. Perhaps when I had a better handle on my abilities, I would be more willing to jump into these paranormal problems. God knew there were plenty of them.

"Phi and I made sure the barn is organized. And Phi set out some options we thought would be nice to have." I checked my watch. "She should be here any minute. Is it weird to you that she will look at you as her alpha?"

Lia shoved me in the shoulder. "I'm not her anything. And, yeah, it's insane. The way they look at us now is eerie. Contempt I get, but this reverence is completely foreign."

I had to agree with her on that. They didn't look at me with nearly as much idolization, but it wasn't as if I was just another woman joining the pack, either. "I wonder if that will change if we don't mate the guys soon. I know I'm not ready for that, yet."

Lia shivered as she placed the basket next to the barn. "I'm not ready, either. Things are perfect right now. Honestly, I'm not sure I'll ever want them to change. And Lucas is okay with that."

I opened both doors, letting the natural light inside. "Noah, too. He said he never wants to break up the twisted sisters. He's the first guy to get how important you guys are to me."

Lia lifted a hand to cover her eyes. I followed her gaze

and watched a car park in the parking lot. "Show time," I muttered moving forward to greet the beautiful shifter.

Dakota and Dreya came out of the main house holding a tray with a pitcher of lemonade and some glasses. Lia and I stopped next to them as Stasia joined us. I extended my hand. "Thanks for coming out to meet with us. It's easier for you to look through our selections."

Stasia smiled revealing even white teeth before she pulled each of us into a hug. "I am so excited the alpha and beta's mates are doing this party. It'll mean even more to my parents."

I kept my smile firmly in place while my stomach turned. Her sentiment added pressure to the relationship I had with Noah. There were so many people invested in us already. What if we didn't work out? Let's face it. In my world shit didn't last all that long. It was inevitable that the guy would cheat, become abusive, or just plain lazy. But Noah was different. He'd never do that to me. And I still couldn't trust that we'd work out as a forever couple.

I gestured to the barn a few feet behind us. "Let's start in here. We have the centerpieces, glasses, and signs in this location. And along one wall are the linen choices. Do you have a look and feel in mind?"

Stasia's brown gaze swiveled around the shelves of our barn where we stored our supplies. Her long blonde hair had loose curls and bounced on her shoulders as she moved. "I was thinking of the traditional gold and black color scheme. My mom loves gold and black, it's classy."

Thank sweet baby Jesus she went with a mundie traditional color palate. I'd already come up with countless ideas. "Perfect. I have several ideas that I'd like to show you before you look through what we have."

Kota placed the lemonade on a table. "Would you like a

cold drink. It's hot in here. We haven't installed an air conditioner, yet."

Stasia took the glass Dreya was holding for her. "Thank you." She took a sip and her eyes went wide. "Oh, this is delicious. We have to have this at the party. My dad loves fresh lemonade."

"We can do that," Dakota assured her.

I pulled the backdrop we'd used for the Roaring Twenties party we'd thrown for Albar, a gargoyle and broker who promised to be a repeat client, out of the aisle where we'd stored it. "I'm thinking we use this for a photo booth. The gold glitter waterfall on the black background is exquisite. Lia will make some props on the laser, like the numbers five and zero on a stick that someone can hold up like glasses."

"We have the gold and black boas and black top hats, as well," Kota added.

We would be able to reuse a significant number of the items we'd used for Albar's party, given the similar color schemes. We used to have a much harder time using stuff a second or third time because it wasn't organized very well, and was difficult to locate between the four crammed storage sheds that we'd used before purchasing the plantation.

Stasia bounced over to the panel and ran a hand down the surface. "I absolutely love this. It's going to be so elegant. Just what my parents deserve."

I beamed at her approval, then gestured to the table we had set up before Phi left to teach her class. "We took the liberty of putting together one of our ideas for a table setting over here."

"That centerpiece is perfect, but I don't like the cream-colored tablecloth. I was thinking perhaps white or black. Still neutral," Stasia said as she looked over the table.

I was glad she liked the centerpiece. It was my favorite. We'd used a tall glass hurricane and tossed in whicker balls, gold balls, and other shapes with white lights strung throughout the objects.

Stasia picked up the silverware and set it next to the plate. "I can't believe I can choose real silverware and plates. We've always used disposable stuff. And, I was thinking of having a sweet's cart rather than a cake. My family likes too many desserts for us to choose just one."

Lia gestured to a back corner where we had a wooden cart Phi's husband made as a dessert display for parties. It had large wooden wheels and handles but it wasn't really meant to be pushed around. The top was at counter height with two sections positioned at bar height on each end. "We often use this when we have a large dessert selection. The top canopy can be changed to gold to match the décor and I can create a new sign for the back. Something that represents your parents."

Dreya gestured to the large panel that said, 'dessert bar because love is sweet.' "It would be great to create a wallpaper using pictures from their life together. We could add a saying above that, or not."

Stasia's eyes filled with tears and she waved a hand frantically in front of her eyes. "Oh my gosh! I am going to have a video done to show everyone. I like this idea, too, because maybe it could be something they could take with them."

My mind started whirling through countless ideas that we could do with pictures. "We've done the pictures on four-foot-tall numbers. Or we could cut out a massive shape of the state or country where they met and add them to that. Make the display more meaningful to them."

Dakota pursed her lips as she stared at the panel attached to the sweet cart. "A perfect rectangle would look better attached to this. The shape would be better as a keepsake. I'd love something like that."

Stasia agreed with Kota and decided to use a cutout of

Louisiana for the pictures. Lia offered to shellac the pictures to the cutout so that the piece lasted forever. We went over the rest of the details and finalized her choice for engraving on the wine glasses she'd selected.

"We need you to let us know who will be catering the event before you go. And, would you like us to ask Brezok to be the bartender? Or did you have someone else in mind?" Lia asked.

Stasia pulled her phone out. "I haven't finalized the food yet. I was hoping for someone that could bring wood fired pizzas. My parents went to North Carolina several years back and ate at a restaurant that served them near their Air BNB. They still talk about it."

"Have they eaten at Hot Stone? Lucas and I ate there last night," Lia relayed. "I tried to talk Nigel into branching out and coming here for our monthly ghost tours."

Kota nodded her head. "I'm going to try that starter later this week. It's time we put that pizza oven to use. I'd offer to try and make them but that's too much work for us to take on with everything else."

Stasia chewed on the corner of her lip. "They love Hot Stone and go there once a week. I'll talk to Nigel and find out if we can place a big order. If you guys have an oven that the pack can use to reheat them, it won't matter if they get cold."

I didn't like not having answers, given the event was less than two weeks away. I allowed Lia to take over at this point as I struggled to restrain my desire to force Stasia to make a decision. It gave me the hives to have something as big as food up in the air with so little time left. As my sisters had told me before, I had to let shit like that go. Stasia asked us to have Brezok there, then took her leave to go and visit Nigel.

Lia made notes in her phone to send to Phi, who would make a master sheet of what needed to be done. I grabbed a glass of lemonade and carried it outside when I heard Noah and Lucas calling for us. A smile spread over my face when Noah wrapped me in a hug and kissed me. I swooned as if I was a love-sick schoolgirl.

"Hey." I ran my hands over his shoulders.

Noah chuckled and bopped the end of my nose. "Hey, you."

Steve popped his head out of the main house. "The last tour is gone, and dinner is ready. Cami is changing out of her costume. Are you guys ready to eat?"

Kota set the lemonade on one of the two the tables under the port cochere. "I could eat. Jeff is on his way over to join us. He got done with his calls early."

Within thirty minutes we were all sitting down to eat. Noah and Lucas had become regulars at our dinner table and stayed at the plantation a few nights a week.

Lia popped a hush puppy into her mouth. "How did the tour go today, Cami? Are you still enjoying them?"

The former ghoul's eyes lit up. "It was fun. I enjoy sharing what life was like back then. It's refreshing to see the horror on mundie faces when I describe the life of a slave. It gives me hope that things won't revert to how they used to be. It also helps that the visitors can't see my mom."

Lucas shuddered and shook his head. "That's the one thing I've had a hard time getting used to about this place. I've never cared for ghosts, but she freaks me out when she hovers and watches you all the time. I can feel her longing."

Cami's cheeks pinkened. "She would never have gotten away with that before. I don't have the heart to tell her to leave me alone when it feels good to see her concern for me. I'll tell her to be less conspicuous."

Lucas held up his hand. "Don't do anything of the sort. This is a journey the two of you have to go through to reconnect and I don't want to stand in the way. Just don't take it personal if I avoid her."

Lia chuckled and patted Lucas's shoulder. "Is the big bad alpha afraid of a little ghost?"

"You're damn right I am," Lucas admitted. "I'd rather face another barghest."

I tensed when he mentioned the Fae creature that had attacked them in the French Quarter the night before. Jeff set his beer down. "I might be out of line here, but have you called Phoebe about that? Isn't she like the head person in the magical world?"

That wasn't a bad idea. I wanted to avoid it altogether but that wasn't realistic. "I bet she could tell us where it came from at least."

Dreya pulled out her phone and hit Phoebe's contact, putting it on speaker. It rang twice before she answered. "Phoebe. It's Dreya from the Six Twisted Sisters in New Orleans. Dahlia, Dani and Dakota are here with me. So are our mates. Anyway, we were hoping you could help us with an issue."

"Yes. The party planners. I still need to talk to you about Nina's seventeenth birthday party but not right now. How can I help you?" Phoebe asked.

Dre nodded to Lia who took a deep breath and told her about the encounter they'd had with the barghest the night before. Lucas added what he saw as well.

"Fae can only come through in England and none have passed through in months according to Fiona. Although, I was gone in the Underworld recently and she was in Eidothea, which is the Fae realm, to help her friend have her dragon baby. I haven't talked to her, but it seems unlikely anything would have gotten through during that time." Phoebe informed them.

My stomach cramped as I considered both of them being off the planet at the same time. That screamed disaster to me. "Can you talk to Fiona about the possibility of a secret population of Dark Fae on Earth? We need to know what we're looking at here."

"I'll call her first thing in the morning," Phoebe agreed.

"Thank you. And can you send us any thoughts Nina might have for her party? I can get started on ideas, that way when you're ready we can do it on short notice."

"That would be perfect. I'm afraid my life hasn't allowed me to make many plans. The magical world tends to take up all my time and the last thing I want is to let her down again," Phoebe admitted.

Dreya and Dakota shared their sentiments with her before we thanked her and hung up. Despite me wanting to shove the attack to the backburner, it didn't seem like it would be possible. I felt a lot better having the actual portal guardian looking into any Fae that might have crossed while she was in Eidothea.

I didn't understand how it worked when Fiona was away from the portal, but she should know. I prayed this was a one-time thing and we weren't looking at something bigger like Lia suspected.

CHAPTER 3

DAHLIA

"Is that Lucinda?" I hissed at Dani as we walked from my car to the craft store to buy supplies.

Dani turned in a circle searching the parking lot. "What? Where?"

I grabbed her shoulders and turned her in the direction I swore I saw the red-haired mambo. Only, now that I looked again, the woman that I thought I'd seen was gone. "Nowhere I guess." I was being paranoid. Lucinda was in Coldwater Correctional Center paying for her crimes.

Dani patted my shoulder and continued toward the entrance. "She's not going to bother us anymore. She was taken into custody."

"You're right. I must have been seeing things." If anyone had been standing where I thought I saw Lucinda, they would be somewhere in the area. It was too far from the store and the few cars that were around were empty.

It was unnerving because this was the fifth or sixth time

that I swore I'd seen Lucinda or Rachelle over the past few weeks. Both of the mambos had been arrested by the paranormal police. I couldn't stop wondering if the women could have escaped custody. I barely paid attention as we made our way through the store, grabbing what we needed. It would be stupid to assume it was impossible for the powerful mambos to be contained forever. Then again, Lucas assured me Coldwater was able to imprison any supernatural being, so they had to have special precautions. *You have to let that go. Marie knows you have powerful allies and isn't going to make another move anytime soon.*

Shaking off those thoughts, I looked at Dani as she held up a bag and shook it from side to side. "What do you think of this color balloon? I want to do something different than we did for Albar. Stasia's parents deserve something unique."

I rolled my eyes at my sister as I took a moment before I responded. I never saw the minute differences Dani did at this stage of the game. Dakota would have, but I had no talent for this kind of thing. "Umm, I agree that they need something that's theirs, but I can't tell the difference between that color and this one. You know I need a designer for dummies handbook." I picked up another bag and wiggled it.

Dani sighed as she tossed the bag in her hand into the cart. "You're better than you give yourself credit for. Your problem is you don't stop racing through your to-do list long enough to actually consider things."

An ache bloomed in my chest. Dani was right. I was a doer and always busy getting shit done. If there was a task to do, I was on it and didn't stop until I was finished. I hated waiting until the last minute. And I couldn't sit still when I knew there was more that had to be done.

I placed a hand on her shoulder when she went to move on to the next aisle. "I'm sorry. You're right. I have the list Phi sent us and I've been on a mission to check off all the items.

Would you show me the grouping together? It'll help me be able to visualize the changes you are asking about."

Dani smiled and grabbed several bags from the cart. She tore small holes in each of them and pulled out a balloon then placed them all in my hand. "I'm going to blow these up a little to give you a better idea. Can you get the idea with one of each color? Or should I do more?"

"One of each is fine. I may have been fired from the balloon arches, but I know there will be a grand pattern and plan for it. It'll help to see the choices."

Dani laughed at me then blew up one of the balloons and held it closed with her free hand. I thought about how grateful I was that Deandra had fired me from anything to do with the intricate arches. Apparently, I over inflated them and didn't put the right sizes together for Dea to string together into an arch.

I never imagined how much work went into a balloon arch. It took hours, yet having one made a huge difference. We'd thrown a couple of garden parties where we created a backdrop of paper flowers which turned out gorgeous but didn't make nearly as big of a statement as the balloons. And, oh boy talk about work, those flowers took even longer.

A lady walking down the aisle with a friend glared at us while Dani blew into the latex. "I wish some stores were more selective with their clientele."

I smiled at her and waved. "You're in a major craft store, not Nieman Marcus. And we're trying to decide which gold to use for an arch for a fiftieth wedding anniversary, not eating dinner in the middle of an aisle."

The lady's friend gaped at me while the woman sniffed and moved on making Dani and I burst out laughing. Dani let go of the third balloon she'd blown up and it sailed through the air making farting noises as it went. Our laughter increased until we were wiping tears from the corners of our eyes.

"Did you see their faces when you said that?" Dani grabbed another gold balloon and blew into it.

I nodded and watched as she held the four that she'd expanded together. "That made my day. And I can see what you mean about the difference now."

Dani grabbed the bag she'd been debating over from the hook and took one out. "I'm going to try one of these and see if it'll be better. We might as well be sure."

I pulled my cell phone from my purse and snapped a picture of what she held in her hands. "I'm sending this to the others so they can weigh in, as well. I actually like both golds. One is pearlescent while the other is metallic. You wouldn't need many of the last one. Then again, I'm no good at this stuff, so I could be wrong."

Dani held onto the latex as she slowly let the air out and put them back in their bags. "I actually like your suggestion. I'm going to grab a bag so we can add a few in here and there and if anyone thinks there should be more then we can pick up some more. What else do we need?"

I pulled up the list from Phi and scanned it. "We need some more greenery for the crescent moon thing she is doing for the haunted tour."

Dani's forehead furrowed as she leaned closer to me and looked at the thumbnail Phi included so we understood what she needed. "That's right. I told her we needed to string lights through this. We can add different flowers throughout each month. Has Tucker cut out the shape already?"

I lifted a shoulder. "Yeah. He did it Sunday when he was in the shop with us. It's propped to the right of the jigsaw. Why?"

Dani pushed the cart to the other side of the store. "Because I was going to start attaching the greenery to it.

This is going to be a nice piece to have. The next baby shower we have scheduled is debating between the chunky rainbows and flowers. Either way she goes, we can use this for that event, too."

I picked up some fake boxwood. "What do you think of using this? It's not the eucalyptus look. I don't see anything that is of decent quality."

Dani shook her head. "The boxwood won't work if she already has some. Let's check the garland. It'll be harder to work with than the stems. However, there are usually some that look great."

We found what we were looking for among the fake garlands and went to the front to check out. I stuffed my cell phone in my back pocket and grabbed the company credit card to pay for our goods. Dani pushed the cart across the parking lot while I retrieved my keys from the bottom of the abyss known as my handbag. Like many women my age I carried a big purse. It was a holdover from the days of having to carry an assortment of stuff for my kids.

"Aha!" I declared in triumph as I lofted my catch in the air.

Dani chuckled. "This is why I never carry a purse. I would never find anything."

I snorted. I'd become accustomed to having Dani toss her wallet and phone in my purse when we went out. See? There was still a reason I needed a big bag. I popped the backend and we put the bags in the vehicle. Something slammed into the back of my skull, making me stumble forward and drop my purse onto the pavement.

What the hell was that? My head throbbed almost as bad as the time the skin walker threw me against the side of a building giving me an acute subdural hematoma. I'd nearly died. Thankfully, it wasn't that bad this time. But I had no idea what was happening. Where was my sister? I turned my head and caught sight of the shopping cart rolling toward a black sedan parked across from us.

My mind was fuzzy making it hard to process our situation and fight back. A hairy arm wrapped around my chest a split second later. Whoever held me, tightened their limb around my rib cage. It must have been whoever hit me over the head. Based on the black hair, it wasn't Lucinda. She was a red head.

I turned when Dani screamed, but didn't see her. The air next to us shimmered like asphalt on a hot summer day. I opened my mouth to add my screams for help when I felt a tug in my midsection. The last thing I saw before the bright sunshine disappeared was my purse on the ground behind the rear end of my SUV. The trunk was open with all of our packages sitting there like birds on a wire watching our abduction.

The breath was sucked out of me as I was pulled through pitch black. It felt like I was pulled a thousand feet but couldn't tell with nothing to gauge it but the feeling of moving. When lights started streaking past me like I was on the Millennium Falcon and we'd just gotten to light speed, I thought I was going to throw up. That was only made worse when the hairy appendage tightened around my abdomen.

All movement stopped and I became weightless for a split second before I dropped to a hard stone floor. My knee hit first, making me curse. I felt like I was still on whatever roller coaster I had just been on, so I remained in place. The last thing I needed was to fall on my face. A body landed next to me. I immediately recognized Dani's dark blonde hair. I scrambled to her side. Something magical had just snatched us out of a busy parking lot. I felt my phone in my back pocket, but I was pretty sure it broke when my big butt came down on it. My heart galloped into my throat. Whoever did this was extremely powerful meaning we were fucked.

"Where are we?" Dani whispered.

The sound of water dripping in the distance didn't give me a clue about where we were at. I wanted to say underground, but it could be a leaky faucet. As my eyes started to adjust, I caught sight of the rough stone walls. "I think we're underground." I continued my assessment. It smelled like musty earth, too.

I sensed Kaitlyn's magic. I wondered what that was about. Had she kidnapped us? That made no sense. She wouldn't do something like that to us. My eyes were starting to adjust to the darkness when light exploded from an overhead structure and a television turned on to the show Bones. It was fitting for a woman whose décor consisted of skulls, femurs, fingers and more.

I scrambled to my feet, pulling Dani up with me. We really were screwed. Marie Laveau was behind our kidnapping. We'd been taken to a colorful living room with colorful couches and a large rug on the stone floor. I expected a dungeon and torture chamber.

Instead, herbs and incense filled the area along with countless bottles. Some held chicken feet while others had colorful liquids in them. I met the sneer on Marie's beautiful brown face. Her black hair was covered by a purple tignon she wore on her head. Her blouse and skirt were both loose fitting. She looked like a gypsy not an angry Queen of Voodoo.

"Why did you bring us here?" I demanded. I figured she'd seen enough of my fear. I refused to feed into her demented view that she should rule the entire area without question. She managed to get as far as she had through intimidation and force.

Marie lifted one corner of her full mouth, narrowing her eyes as she glared daggers at us. "To make you pay for ruining my plans. The only reason I'm standing here right

FRENCH QUARTER FAE

now is because your head witch created wards blocking gods from my lair. But I can't leave here if the loa start torturing me. And it's all because of you and your sisters."

I returned her look and added an extra layer of disgust. "Our mates will come looking for us and they'll make you regret laying a hand on our heads. And if our stuff was stolen, I will personally drag you out of this pit and leave you to your pissed-off gods."

Laveau threw her head back and started laughing. I looked at Dani whose expression reflected the question I was wondering. Was she going to kill us now? Was that why she thought that was funny.

Marie sobered and moved to a bookcase. "Your mates will find empty husks by the time they find you." The Voodoo Queen grabbed a jar and pulled the cork from the top then poured some powder in her palm. It looked like glitter. I really hoped it wasn't actually the sparkly crap. That was the herpes of arts and craft. It got everywhere and was impossible to clean off of yourself or anything else.

When Marie started chanting in Creole, the hairs on my body stood on end. I take that last thought back. I would gladly accept glitter. I moved closer to Dani at the same time Marie held her hand out and blew the powder into our faces. My hands flew up and my eyes slammed shut. A few particles managed to land on my irises with the rest coating my skin. When I gasped it went up my nose and down my throat.

At first nothing happened aside from me having to steady myself. When I blinked and opened my eyes a scream left my mouth when my gaze landed on Dani. She'd aged years in a matter of seconds. Dani started swatting at her arms, chest and torso. "What's happening?"

Marie stared stonily at us. "I've cursed you to age and die. Like I said, your mates will find nothing but husks."

We could not let that happen. I could feel tiny particles

marching through my blood stream. It was like they were herding my healthy cells to their doom, taking my vitality and youth with them. I wasn't that young to begin with. At forty-five, I had lived half of my life. I wanted to live the rest of it.

I tried to slow my racing heart so I could think about what I could do stop it. The first thought was angel light. Coaxing my rage, I allowed it to take over hoping instinct would take over. Sure enough, a second later light burst from my hands, burning through the powder Marie had used to curse us.

Dani's skin reverted some, but she wasn't back to normal. I couldn't think about that because Marie was screaming at her mambos to do something. Several women came running into the room wearing their ceremonial garb, but they all stopped short when they saw the light.

"We need to cast a protection spell over ourselves," I whispered to Dani.

Dani dipped her head once. "Alright, now before they decide to ignore your light."

I clasped her hand again and concentrated on the barrier I wanted to place over us. This was the one spell we'd practiced most often so it didn't take long for me to have the image of an impenetrable shield around me and Dani. I nodded at Dani and together we chanted the spell under our breaths.

Marie finally gave up on her mambos and ran at us. I cringed but held my stance with Dani. It would hurt if she knocked us over, but I needed to hold firm. A laugh bubbled out of me when Marie stopped abruptly and jerked back as if she slammed into a brick wall.

"I will break down whatever ward you have over yourselves. You are not going to win this," Marie yelled at us.

The Queen of Voodoo turned and tossed black energy at

her television blowing it to bits right when Temperance and Booth were about to have their baby. Her tirade continued as she destroyed a chair sending bits of cotton fluff flying throughout the room. She grabbed a skull and threw it at us. It shattered when it hit my barrier. We watched as she continued throwing shit around. It seemed like forever before she finally settled down and stopped.

Marie's beautiful features twisted with anger as she leaned into our faces. "I will find a way to make you bitches pay for what you have done to my life. You *never* mess with the Queen of Voodoo! Everyone in New Orleans knows that. Except the six of you. I might not be able to reach the other four yet, but I will get past whatever you two are doing and get the others."

I watched the queen's spit slide down the magical shield while trying to hide the way I was trembling from head to toe. I was one second from passing out and I had no idea how Dani and I had managed to stop her attack.

Dani clutched my hand tighter as the Queen of Voodoo stalked off to regroup. Neither of us said a word, both of us too lost in our thoughts. I wanted to apologize to my sister. I felt responsible because I was the one to put us in a position against Marie in the first place. I know Dani would rather focus on events and things that put a smile on people's faces.

Reminding myself that I wasn't responsible for Marie's crazy didn't help alleviate the knot in my stomach. I'd wait to tell her I was sorry. I had to get us out of there first.

CHAPTER 4

DANIELLE

Fear and anger made tears prickle the back of my eyes. "How the hell are we going to get out of this?" My words lashed out at my sister with razor sharp barbs.

I didn't blame Lia for our current predicament. I was terrified and pissed. I'd been trying to straddle the line between the mundie and magical worlds from the beginning. It was difficult to join the magical community all-in like some of my sisters already had. They were far better at dealing with the differences between their two worlds. I was now determined to put more effort into my magic. If I got better at using my psychometry and other skills, I wouldn't be as reluctant.

People like Marie Laveau had to be stopped. I couldn't stand the thought of her getting away with shit like this and using it to manipulate the magical world. One thing Lia had shared with the rest of us was a dislike of the powerful using their position to take advantage of others.

I didn't want to live under her thumb. Around seventy percent of our clients were paranormal. While none of our families had yet shown signs of having powers, that could change. No one knew how far-reaching Phoebe's spell was or how long it might take to activate in our brothers and children.

Lia dropped her head against the wall and shot me an apologetic look. "I have no answers right now. We should be safe for the time being. I can feel our magic working together to keep Marie's efforts at bay. My first thought is to try and destroy both Marie and Kaitlyn's wards. We need to be able to send a signal out. And if the loa were able to reach Marie here then perhaps it would distract her enough for us to escape."

I rattled the chains running from the cuffs around my wrists to an anchor in the stone wall behind us. "That's a good start and given that I have nothing at the moment, I'm willing to try that. Do you know how our power got braided together? If we understood that, we could join our efforts again against the wards. Our protection is so tightly wound together it isn't allowing one spec of Marie's curse through."

That had been the most terrifying few minutes of my life. When Marie had cast that aging curse and I saw Lia age a decade in the blink of an eye, I thought we were done for. Thanks to Lia's fast thinking, we didn't succumb. The fact that I had the same thought almost as fast as she did, let me know I was better equipped to handle these crises than I previously believed.

Lia's forehead furrowed, although it wasn't as evident given that the wrinkles that she'd gained from Marie's spell hadn't vanished entirely. "I have no idea why it did that. My best guess is that it's courtesy of our bond. The six of us share a connection that's deep and abiding no matter how much we might annoy each other. Mom always used to say we had to love each other because family were the ones you could count on to be there for you."

I used to think it was our mom's way of trying to keep the peace in a house with ten children. The six of us have had our differences over the years, yet we've always come back to each other. And my sisters have been there for me any time I've needed them. Lia was right. Like many sisters, we had a special bond. We rallied and came together, regardless of any petty differences. So many examples rushed through my mind at that moment. From the time Phi was diagnosed with breast cancer to the time that Leo died to the time that my daughter got married.

Filled with the love we shared, I nodded. "Let's try it." I immediately started working on my intent to wipe away Marie and Kaitlyn's wards. The steps to casting and magic came as if I'd done it far longer than a hand full of months.

I reached out and twined my fingers with Lia's and nodded to let her know I was ready. Together we chanted, *"Perdere."* Energy trickled from us, and I felt my energy join Lia's.

I sat up on my knees as I waited for it to destroy the wards. Lia leaned forward and scanned for a sign it had worked. Aside from feeling the energy leave us, there was no other indication that we had done anything.

I couldn't stand this waiting. Unfortunately, I wasn't certain what should have happened. "Do you think it worked?"

Dahlia cocked her head to the side and lifted a shoulder. "You should use your psychometry on the stones to see if you can still feel it."

I'd been spending all of my energy trying to keep my ability under wraps. The thought of using it scared me. I got sucked into the memories when I touched stuff. I was completely out of control and immersed in the emotions of the person. That was a lot of baggage I didn't need to add to my own. I had enough to deal with.

Lia squeezed my hand. "You can't keep hiding from it, Dani. This is no way to live. I'm no expert but as I've tried to take control of my visions, I've been thinking of ways you might be able to handle yours. You can't always wear gloves or walk around with your hands under your arms or in your pockets. What if you force your mind to remain above the memories? Kinda like when you worked nights and kept your fatigue at bay while also doing your job. You are uniquely skilled in that regard, so I thought you could adapt that and use it to your advantage."

A smile spread across my face as I listened to Lia. Her idea was brilliant. It had taken me years to teach myself how to work nights and not lose my entire life to sleep. Fatigue was a buzz in the back of my mind while I did what I needed to do. Of course, eventually I had to give in and sleep, but I managed well enough. "It's the best idea I've heard in a long time. I'll give it a try."

I pulled my fingers out of her hold and wiggled them as I looked around for the best place to touch the wall. Locations that were touched more often carried a stronger psychic imprint and would give me more information. There had to be places that would have heavier wards.

The cell was small, damp and dark. My eyes had had enough time to adjust to the low lighting that came from under the panel that acted as the door. The space was carved out of the earth in Marie's underground lair. There was nothing in the room aside from a few bolts in the wall and us. The ground was muddy and there was mold somewhere based on the way the place smelled, but there was nothing else.

Deciding the outer wall was my best bet, I crawled through the mud grimacing at the way it squished between my fingers and stopped at the opposite side of the room from the entrance. Lia scurried to join me and laid a hand on my shoulder, letting me know she was there for me.

"Pull me out if I get stuck," I told her. It was one of my fears when I was sucked into a memory.

Lia smiled and nodded. "You can count on it. I'll give you a minute. That should be long enough to tell if the wards are still up."

I jolted as I laid my hand on the cool stone. The memory of a woman digging into the stone and dirt tried to suck me under and I pushed that aside, skimming past it as I searched for the energy of the wards. I wasn't exactly sure what I was looking for until I came up against a massive blockade. It was like a steel barrier surrounding us.

My stomach churned as I slumped. "It didn't work. Those are some powerful wards. We're going to freaking die down here. Shit." Tears burned my eyes as I fought against the despair threatening to drown me.

Dahlia sighed as she hugged me to her. "We aren't going to die down here. This isn't how our story ends, sestra. Dre and Kota will already be looking for us and they will call Lucas and Noah. We have a huge support network. We just need to find a way around these wards to send them a hint as to our location. No one can scry for us because of Laveau's wards."

I lifted my hands and let them drop back into my lap. The defeat making me feel as if I had a thousand-pound weight on me. "I'm open to suggestions. We're surrounded by her power."

Lia's gaze moved around our cell before landing on her lap. "Was the strength equal all around us?" She lifted her brown eyes to mine.

FRENCH QUARTER FAE

My mouth parted as I realized what she asking. "I didn't pay attention to what was beneath us. I'll check that." If it was possible to get past the ward below us, we might be able to reach our sisters and be rescued.

I took a deep breath to ready myself then placed my hand on the wall. A whoop almost slipped past my lips when I was able to keep the memories from flooding my mind. It was easy to stick to the surface of them while remaining focused on the energy of the wards. When I encountered the thick wall of Marie's, I followed it down. My heart sped up and a smile crossed my face.

I dropped my hand and grabbed Lia's arm. "It feels like a thin membrane beneath us as opposed to the thick steel wall all around and above us. How do we exploit that?"

Dahlia turned her back to the entrance and started digging into the mud. "We need to dig down through the dirt beneath us. If my theory is right then we can get beneath the ward that is blocking anyone from finding us, giving our sisters and Kaitlyn a chance to find and rescue us."

Her excitement fed into my own and my mind started working through the possibilities. "I say we prod them, as well. A little poke in the ass to focus the energy I know they have working to locate us."

"God bless it. We're going to get the hell out of here," Lia exclaimed as she continued digging.

"Ugh. This is slimier than I would have expected." I yelped and pulled my hands out of the dirt. Bile rose in my throat when something plopped into the pile I'd pushed out of the hole.

"What is that?" Lia leaned closer then picked up the object and wiped the mud off of it. Lia's face lost color as she tossed the object away from her. "That was some kind of a bone. I don't know if I can do this."

My heart settled hearing her say it was a bone. I could

deal with that much easier than if it was some kind of super bug. As a nurse I'd dealt with death and every fluid a body could produce. "We need to dig deeper. Can you feel the energy of the ward? I don't feel much aside from the low-level buzz."

"Same here. How are you not bothered by the fact that we are likely sifting through human remains? I feel like I might puke." Lia shuddered and shook her head from side to side.

The sound of metal creaking made both of us jump. The door panel was moving. Lia and I turned around and positioned our bodies in front of the hole we had dug. It wasn't all that deep. However, it was clear we were trying to do something. I didn't want Marie moving us to a location where we wouldn't be able to try and dig past the wards. Doing so was our best bet.

Light from the room outside illuminated the empty space where we'd been held. Marie's beautiful face came into view as the panel opened further. A younger version of herself was standing next to her. They both had on loose, colorful clothing. Marie had on a skirt and peasant type blouse while her daughter wore linen pants and a cotton top. Where Marie had a traditional tignon on her head, the younger woman did not. Her long black hair hung in loose curls to the middle of her back.

Marie sashayed into the room, her ankle boots sinking into the mud a few centimeters. You'd think she would tiptoe or hesitate, but she moved with certainty and purpose, completely unbothered by the mud. "I thought I would take a page out of your book and join powers with my daughter to break you two."

That explained why the young woman looked like Marie. It was her heir. Lia gestured to the pair. "Are you training her to become the next Queen of Voodoo? Maybe she'll do a better job."

FRENCH QUARTER FAE

Marie snarled and bent over, putting her in Dahlia's face. "You're messing with the wrong Queen, bitch!"

Marie's daughter put her hand on Marie's back. "I'm eager to join our powers so you can teach these witches a lesson, mom." At first, I thought the daughter was trying to settle her mom. Then I felt the hum of death and saw her creepy smile. Crazy must be bred into their DNA.

Marie straightened and brushed her hands down the front of her blouse before she extended her hand to her daughter. Her fingers closed on her daughter's and the two started breathing together. Their gazes went distant and then the chanting began. Their words made the hair on the back of my neck prickle at the same time bile filled my mouth. The air waivered around the two of them as their energy built.

Dahlia shot me a wide-eyed look and the two of us backed up until our asses were sitting in the hole and our backs were presses against the wall. "How do we send more power to our protection?" I hissed at Lia.

Lia's large brown eyes were frantic when they shifted my way. "I've got no idea. Concentrate on our protection and repelling their spells?"

I nodded and did as she suggested even though her question denoted doubt. It was actually a solid suggestion. One I would have thought of if I hadn't been so busy panicking. The oily feel of their magic lessened the more I thought about repelling them.

I screamed when sparks were generated an inch from my eyebrows. I was thrown backward at the same time. Grabbing for Dahlia, I clung to her as the sparks continued for several seconds before they traveled all over me. As suddenly as the energy appeared, it ended.

Marie let go of her daughter, lifted her hands and brought them down, pointing in our direction. Black lightning shot from her. It bounced off of an invisible barrier then shot past her daughter's face. Glass shattered somewhere in Marie's living room. Smoke filtered into the cell, adding to the musty scent of the place.

Marie dropped her hands and took several deep breaths. I could see her calming herself down with each inhale and exhale. She was a control freak that didn't like having a break down like this. "This isn't over. I will find a way to get past those protections."

Marie had a scowl on her face as she gestured for her daughter to leave the room. "I lost a Dark Fae ally. That's another sin to be laid at your feet, bitches. You aren't going to like it when I make it past your protections."

Marie's daughter stood by the door listening intently while I bit my tongue to keep from shooting a retort at the vile woman. How the hell were we responsible for the loss of an ally. Could it have been the creature Lucas had killed a couple of nights before? It didn't seem like the beast was capable of sentient thought, let alone speech. With one last glare, Marie slammed the panel closed, plunging us into darkness again.

I crawled toward the door the second Marie and her daughter left. It was disgusting to watch Marie creating a replica of herself to take over when she was no longer able to be the reigning Queen of Voodoo. I wanted to hear what they were saying. I expected her to shoot us then dump us in the bayou somewhere, but she hadn't. She had something else in mind.

Dahlia copied my movements and pressed her ear to the panel that served as a door. "How did you manage to find the Dark Fae and ally with them? A Laveau has never done so before."

To our benefit, Marie didn't realize she was still close enough for us to hear. "I felt a thinning of the veils all around

FRENCH QUARTER FAE

the quarter the day of second line parade. I'm certain those idiotic sisters did something when they thwarted Samedi, so I decided to take advantage. You must always be vigilant and prepared to act. Opportunities sprout up when you least expect it. Our family is obligated to the loa. We cannot let these witches win. I will never accept defeat and neither should you."

"How did you pull them through when you sensed the opportunity? I want to be prepared should I ever encounter the same thing." The daughter sounded like a sycophant.

The sound of pans clattering echoed through the space as the sound of their footsteps retreated. I prayed they would stay close enough for us to hear. "I was trying to bring more loa through to appease Samedi. It was pure luck when I made contact with Dark Fae instead. They've wanted to come to this world and get revenge against a group of witches in England. I used the opportunity to strike a bargain with them. They'll be my personal..." Marie's words were drowned out by the sound of a faucet turning on.

Lia and I remained pressed to the door but we didn't hear anything else. At least we understood how the barghest happened to be in New Orleans. I came to terms, in that dank smelly cell, that this was our life. Fate had given us more than the plantation the day we signed the loan papers. We were now private detectives for the magical world. It sucked in many ways and it wasn't part of my life plan. That didn't mean I had to be miserable. Life had never been better, even with these chaotic cases. Now all we needed to do was reach our sisters so they could rescue us.

CHAPTER 5

DAHLIA

"How deep do you think we have to dig. I swear we unearthed the previous eight or nine Marie Laveaus." Burials in New Orleans were different. When someone passed on, they were added to the family vault for a year and a day and then brought back to join their ancestors at the back and base of the structure. The thought grossed me out each time I encountered a bone fragment.

Dani paused to wipe the sweat from her forehead with the back of her hand. "I hope these aren't the previous Voodoo Queens. Otherwise, their power will have seeped deeper into the soil making it impossible to get past."

I shivered and sank back onto my heels. We'd been there for at least a day, but it felt like longer. After Marie and her daughter left, we dug some more then took a nap when the exhaustion refused to let up. They fed us some watery soup a couple of times, paid us a few more visits, and we slept even more times. Without a way to see outside, there was no way to determine how much time had actually passed, however we discovered that the food could pass through because they meant us no harm with it.

Although we kept the hole small, two feet wide by less than a foot tall, it was hard to hide it. I was certain we would be caught during their last visit, but Dani and I had cast an illusion over the area making it look normal. It helped that the section wasn't all that big. We hid it when we sat side by side and had taken to spreading the dirt over the rest of the area so there weren't two piles.

The skin on my fingers was shredded and my back screamed at me when I leaned back over the hole to resume digging. Knock on wood, I hadn't had too many aches and pains in my middle age. However long we'd spent hunched over like this was reminding me I was no longer twenty something and in the best shape of my life. "We will get through the magic. It's just a matter of time."

Dani smiled at me. "You're right. I've run marathons. This is just a much longer race. I just wish we had some water. And a bean burrito."

I chuckled as I steeled myself, put my bloody fingers back into the dirt, and continued shoving mud out of our way. I had so much dirt under my nails, I doubted they'd ever be clean again. I refused to think about the body secretions that had likely seeped through the open wounds. "I would kill for a Rosie's burrito right now. And an energy drink."

Dani groaned as she resumed digging. "A tall boy would be fantastic. I should take this time without to detox completely and stop drinking Pepsi, but I won't. It's mother's milk for me and makes me happy."

"I was thinking the same thing about the energy drinks. Life is too short to deny yourself everything. There's nothing wrong with indulging in a few things. At least that's the excuse I'm using. Oh!" I dug frantically as I felt a change in the energy. "We're almost there."

Dani flung handfuls of mud over her shoulder without care. "Holy shit. I had given up hope of getting through. I was digging because you were. Oh my God. This is going to work."

I tilted my head to look at her. "Damn right it's going to work. We're one third of the Six Twisted Sisters."

It was less than a minute later when my fingers encountered none of the barrier Marie had cast to keep them hidden. Shoving my fingers into the soil, I took several deep breaths. "Okay. Are you ready to do this?"

Dani nodded as she buried her hand up to the middle of her forearm in the mud. "You know it. We're sending out a bat signal, right? I've been thinking. We should focus on the sisters and Noah and Lucas at the same time. It's a risk we might not reach them at all, but I think we need to take the chance. Our mates will be able to help the sisters follow our trail better if they feel it too."

My rational mind told me to keep it simple, that we weren't experienced enough to try and reach so many people at once. I wanted to limit us to Dreya, figuring we'd have more energy to hit her with. However, Dani made a good point. "Alright. We send it to Dre, Kota, Phi, Dea, Noah and Lucas."

I closed my eyes picturing them all sitting around the table talking about where to look for us next. I imagined a light seeping through the soil and traveling to the plantation and wrapping around the six of them. I wanted it to pull them to us before Marie stepped up her game like she'd promised.

Once I had my intent firm in my mind, I lifted my lids and waited for Dani to meet my gaze. When her brown eyes landed on mine, we chanted together. "*Magicae trahentium.*"

The energy burst from us, burning as it exited my injured fingertips. I relished the pain. It told me that we'd done it. We had made it past the magic hiding us. We had a shot at being found now. I poured all the energy I could into reaching my sisters and my mate. It was weird to think about Lucas as a mate. It wasn't an idea I was exposed to growing up. Like so many other things in the magical world, it was something I was learning about. It gave me comfort at that moment to know it meant Lucas and Noah would work as hard, if not harder, than our sisters to find us.

The fatigue that had been riding me sapped my energy before I was ready to give up. I sagged forward, hungrier than I had ever been in my life. I tried to reach for Dani when she slumped next to me. "Do you think they felt that?"

I smiled at my sister and finally reached over to squeeze her hand. The action made my pain double while also calming my racing heart. I wasn't alone in this. "I know they felt it. It's just a matter of time now."

My stomach dropped when I heard the squeak of the door being opened. I didn't have enough power to cast the illusion and I couldn't turn around fast enough to hide the hole. My heart hammered in my chest as the room flooded with light. The two seconds it took to open the panel seemed to drag on forever. It was as if time slowed to a crawl.

The scream that followed chilled my blood. I turned my head to see Marie Laveau flying at me. She wrapped her fist in my hair and yanked me away from the hole we'd dug. "I thought I felt a surge of power a second ago. What the hell have you done? Do you really think you managed to get past my ward? You are being held directly beneath my family's tomb. The magic of generations feeds the power shielding you from being found."

I was relieved when Dani scrambled away, pressing her back against the wall so she was better prepared to protect herself. It was bad enough that my fingers were curled in and frozen in place. The digging had taken its toll and I could hardly move the bloody stumps. Still, I pawed at Marie's arm. "Let me go." I needed to regain my energy stores so I could cast another spell around myself and Dani.

Cold steel pressed against my throat making my head go back to avoid being cut. Marie's breath was hot on the side of my face. "I don't think so, bitch. You and your sisters have caused enough problems. Your little attempt to reach out to your mates will go unanswered. I have every hope that your sisters will come running. I'm planning on it. However, the alpha knows better than to risk his people for two weak witches."

Dani glared at Marie. "You underestimate what we mean to them. They'll come after us. And our sisters won't be coming alone."

"Yeah," I said, picking up where Dani was going with this. I wanted her to take her anger out on me since she already had a hold of my hair and a knife to my throat. "Kaitlyn will back our sisters up and rescue us. You'll regret kidnapping us."

Marie threw back her head and laughed. That laughter was joined by another as her daughter entered and crossed to lift Dani by her hair. I wondered if the younger Laveau even had a mind of her own. "The head witch wouldn't dare come after my mother. Don't you know the power of the enemy you made? My mom can decimate hundreds with one enchantment. Kaitlyn wouldn't put her witches on the chopping block. Neither would the shifters. No woman is worth putting an entire pack at risk The entire city of New Orleans is afraid of us, and for good reason."

Marie inclined her head and lifted the hand holding the knife before she let me go. "You forget the power of the loa we have behind us, daughter. And now we have another powerful ally at our beck and call."

Marie Laveau stalked back to the open door and gestured to someone outside. I prayed she wasn't sending zombies in after us. They would rip us apart before we could blink. Dani and I were both completely powerless at the moment. We'd used all we had to reach out to our family.

To my relief and horror, it wasn't the walking dead that entered but four beautiful people. They were tall with perfect complexions, dark eyes, and lithe builds. Who were these people? Their auras screamed paranormal to my senses while also being completely foreign to me. The look in their eyes carried so much hatred that it made me shiver. Marie must have brain washed them, as well.

Before I could blink the newcomers rushed forward and the next thing I knew I was being held between a man with black hair and a woman with purple hair. I shot wild eyes to my sister, hoping that Dani was alright. She was held between two men, one had ocean blue hair and the other had heather green hair.

Dani's eyes hardened and she jerked her chin to the hole we'd dug. Thank God we were so close because I knew she was telling me to tether my energy to the soil so it could be followed by our sisters and mates. They were our only hope of survival now.

Focusing my intent on leaving a trail to follow like we were Hansel and Gretel lost in the woods, I mouthed a spell. I could have spit with more force than the energy that trickled out of me. Panic choked me when Marie smirked at Dani and me. "That was weak and pathetic. Not even enough to make me worry. I'm going to enjoy this. You bitches have caused enough problems. It's time to remind New Orleans why I am the Queen. Take them to the chamber."

The newcomers inclined their heads and tightened their hold on my upper arms. As if my brain finally kicked into gear, I started fighting them. No way was I going to go willingly. I bucked and kicked and tried yanking my arms from their grasp. It was futile. All I managed to do was make myself more tired. The guy punched me in the side, knocking the breath from me.

Deciding I needed to save my energy, I stopped struggling and scanned the room as they carried me through the space. They kept their bodies between me and the shelves of potions, skulls, and other magical items. There was no way for me to grab hold of anything.

Behind me I could hear Dani struggling. A loud crash and the shattering of glass startled me and my captors. They turned, allowing me to see what had happened. A smile broke out over my face when I saw that Dani had managed to knock over one of the units. The men holding her were covered in various liquids. Of course, she was too, but it was enough to piss Marie off.

Marie stalked to my sister, but I couldn't to see what she did because the man and woman pulled me through a door into a circular chamber that was carved out of rock. Unlike the cell where we'd been held, this one had a stone floor rather than mud. I was tossed onto a rough, hard table and held in place by the man and woman. I wiggled and bucked, resuming my fight. The man did something, and it felt like invisible bands wrapped around my throat, torso, and legs. I couldn't move or I would choke myself.

Helplessness made emotion burn the back of my throat while I watched the other guys carry a soaked Dani into the room. I hadn't seen the second table until they shoved her onto the surface. My eyes filled with tears when I met Dani's terrified gaze. I saw the moment the invisible bands wrapped around her, as well.

Marie's daughter approached Dani and snarled at her.

FRENCH QUARTER FAE

"You almost ruined mom's ritual. Too bad for you it didn't work."

"What ritual? What are you going to do to us?" I understood the frantic tremors in Dani's voice as she spoke. Marie had tried to stick the demented loa, Samedi, into Deandra not that long ago. Was she going to do the same thing to us?

Marie picked up a dagger from a small table set along one wall while her daughter moved on to light torches spread around the room. "You'll see soon enough. You only have yourselves to blame for your predicament. Although, I should thank you for bringing me my Dark Fae allies." So that's what these people were. It was good to know not all of the Dark Fae were ugly monsters.

Something plucked the stream of energy that ran from me to the hole in the other room. It felt like a probe and made my heart race. My tears dried up as hope surged through me. Dani must have felt something similar because a wide smile broke out over her face.

I tried to follow the line of my spell back to the source, but Marie approached me with a knife and a wooden bowl. The dark brown stains on the bowl made my heart race in my chest. "This'll hurt. A lot if I'm lucky," she said before she cut my arm. The wound was shallow and hurt like the dickens, exactly like a paper cut.

"No!" I shouted as Marie crossed to Dani and sliced her in several places on her arms and legs. To her credit, Dani didn't utter a peep.

With a scowl, Marie turned back to me and proceeded to slice me several more times. Her movements got angrier the more she worked. She wanted us to cry out in pain. I locked gazes with Dani for strength as the pain increased with each cut.

Marie set the bowl on the table and proceeded to add several ingredients to the mixture then painted her body with the bloody concoction. She and her daughter started chanting. It seemed like they danced and chanted for an hour before finally stopping. Marie picked up the wooden bowl and threw it against the wall.

Whatever Marie had tried just now didn't work. My insides squirmed like a jar full of worms while my sister was unfazed by the events. Instead, Dani's brow furrowed as she focused on her hands. When her finger flickered into a long, sharp, curved black nail, I realized she was trying to shift any part of her body into her dragon. It would be good is she could manage talons.

"It's good to see some things have stayed the same," I taunted the Queen of Voodoo.

Marie simply scowled at me and crossed to my side. "I might not be able to beat your magic and use your bodies, but I can eliminate the threat you pose to me and my family." That sounded ominous.

My heart jumped into my throat when Marie held out her hand and her daughter slapped the dagger into her palm. Dani's struggles intensified and I looked into her eyes. She mouthed something to me but I couldn't make out what she said. I had to keep my eyes on the nasty woman standing above me.

Marie's smile turned vicious as she lifted the knife above her head. She looked at me for a split second, letting my terror of her intentions sink in. I hated myself for giving her what she wanted, but I couldn't stop the fear from overwhelming me. Marie's smile turned victorious as she slammed her weapon into my chest. I watched as her hand moved slightly before the blade pierced my flesh and cut through muscles, veins and tendons.

Tears filled my eyes as I fought for breath. Dani's screams sounded far away. I wanted to reassure her that we would be alright but I couldn't form words. And even if I could have, I no longer believed them. The knife in my chest was irrevocable proof that I was not going to survive this attack. Marie had won this round. The worst part was Dani was likely to go out with me. And then Marie would stand a chance of regaining the power we'd manage to wrestle from her and more.

With powerful Dark Fae at her side, she was able to reach more people and places. The fear she used to have would return full force.

We had watched our mom suffer from metastatic breast cancer for years and at the end I was both frustrated and awed by her denial that it was going to win. She used to say she was going to beat it no matter what the doctors said. She believed a miracle could happen until the second the cancer finally claimed her.

Our mom's courage and grace inspired me every day. She never gave up, no matter how dire. And neither would I. In the face of my demise, our mom helped me find a shred of hope that refused to be diminished. I prayed to whatever gods were listening to help my sister and I both to survive. We were on our second act in life and finally becoming who we were meant to be. Neither of us were ready to die yet.

As if to claim the shred I was clinging to, the pain in my chest flared. It hurt like the fires of hell were burning through it and I couldn't catch my breath. My heart was beating erratically. Marie had missed that vital organ. That seemed intentional on her part. She was the type of evil that would want me to suffer. That made me even more determined to survive this. I couldn't give up and let her have the satisfaction of watching me die. It wasn't in my DNA.

As hard as I was trying to fight to stay alive, exhaustion was claiming me. The sound of something battering wood overpowered Dani calling out my name. I swear I heard voices shouting and growls filling the room. I managed to turn my head away from Dani's tear-streaked face to see Lucas and a massive stone gargoyle.

I blinked, believing my eyes were playing a trick on me. The world became blurry and unfocused, making it impossible to see anything clearly. All I could make out were shapes rushing about the room. A second later, my eyes slipped closed, plunging me into darkness.

CHAPTER 6

DANIELLE

My heart threatened to jump right out of my ribcage when that knife plunged into my sister's chest. I prayed with all my might that the spell I cast before the weapon pierced my sister's skin worked. When I saw the blade in Marie's hand, I acted on instinct and tried an enchantment that would keep the steel from piercing any of Lia's vital organs. Kip could heal her as long as she wasn't mortally wounded.

Tears burned my eyes and temples as they fell freely. How the hell had this happened? I'd known our situation was dire when we were snatched. Marie's intention to use us to fulfill her promises to her Voodoo gods was obvious from her repeated rantings. For her it was a matter of regaining her position of power and reputation. And it seemed she would stop at nothing.

"No, Lia! Stay with me," I shouted when I noticed Dahlia's eyes slipping closed.

Marie turned around and shot me a victorious grin. "With your sister gone I will be able to put Samedi's soul into your body and give him a chance to once again roam the world."

A sense of satisfaction filled me knowing the connection my sisters and I shared had stopped all of her efforts thus far. I had no idea how long we'd been in there, but our absence had definitely been noticed and the troops rallied. I had no doubt that Dre, Kota, Dea, and Phi were searching along with Noah and Lucas. Those six would never stop looking, no matter what Marie said about Lucas not risking his pack. He loved Dahlia. We just needed to hang on until they found us. Hopefully Lia and I had dug deep enough and the power that I could still feel trickling from both of us could reach our family.

The Dark Fae helping Marie lost their smiles and went on alert. Marie grabbed the knife and pulled it from Lia's chest. My sister didn't even flinch. My heart skipped a beat as a minute smile broke over her face. I turned my head, following her gaze, and cried out in relief. Lucas had broken down the door and was charging toward his mate.

What made the sight so much better was the glimpse I caught of Noah and my sisters behind him. I couldn't tell exactly who was there because an eight-foot-tall gargoyle blocked my view. The stone creature moved with surprising speed for its size. It was also oddly fluid for something made of rock.

Who the hell was the gargoyle? The only one we knew was Albar, the guy we did the Roaring Twenties party for. Whoever it was, had my gratitude. He picked up a mambo that was crouching in the corner of the room muttering something under her breath and waving her arms over her head. Her movements reminded me of the dance I'd seen them do a couple of times. The gargoyle threw the woman against the wall, cutting off her chants.

Screams echoed through the space and for several seconds all I could see were bodies grappling and blood flying. I tried shifting my fingers into talons again. I'd managed it earlier and had started to cut through the rope holding my wrists to the stone table. It was awkward and I'd cut my skin more than the rope. I couldn't let that stop me. I had to get free and help Lia.

I grunted when a body landed on my torso, knocking the breath from me, even though I was lying down and hadn't moved. It was the oddest sensation. The gargoyle was suddenly looking at me with a grimace. At least I thought that was his expression. It was difficult to tell with his harsh features. "Sorry about that. Let me help with those." That voice sounded like a gravelly version of Albar's.

"Albar? Is that you?" I asked.

Albar nodded and the corners of his mouth lifted. It was frightening and looked like he was snarling at me. I jerked my arm back when he reached for it. "Yes. I came when Lucas sent the call out."

My heart slowed when he jerked the rope, tearing it from me. "Tha..." My words were cut off when his stone wings hit the table that I was on because a Dark Fae had attacked him from behind. The roar Albar let out as his weight crushed the Dark Fae harder into my chest rattled my bones. I couldn't breathe and spots danced in the edges of my vision within seconds.

Thankfully, Albar's weight disappeared along with him. He pulled off a move that made my head spin. He lifted off of his feet, flew backward, and turned to take his attacker with him all in the span of one rapid heartbeat. While I could run marathons - as long as I didn't try to chew gum at the same time. I'd never been all that athletic.

My chest ached making me wonder if I had a cracked rib. Using my freed hand, I shoved the Dark Fae off of me before reaching for the other tie. I sucked in a breath when I saw Kota, Dre, Dea, and Phi all facing off with mambos. Given the black aura surrounding Marie's minions, I would say the loa were giving them strength.

Rage crossed Kota's face before a machete appeared in her hand. Ever since the zombie attack that had become her weapon of choice. "You stink, bitch. Get your ugly ass out of my face," Kota shouted as she swung her weapon around. The steel connected with the mambo's side and cut through skin. Blood poured from the wound and sprayed a pissed off Dakota.

I went to work on the knot while searching the room for Noah and Lucas. Albar seemed to be everywhere. Several shifters from the pack were fighting Marie's minions and the Dark Fae. Monsters similar to the one Dahlia described from the Quarter had joined the melee turning the room into a chaotic, bloody mess. Marie and her daughter were huddled together chanting something in a low rhythmic tone.

Phi and Dre ran to me, both panting heavily. Dre reached for the rope. "I've got this, sestra."

A sob escaped me as my tears returned. I hadn't felt the numerous cuts covering my body until that moment. It was like her touch opened the flood gates. "No, forget about me. Help Dahlia. Marie stabbed her in the chest. She could already be dead."

Dre and Phi's eyes went wide. Dre cursed and ran to her side while Phi stood there frozen for a second. It was Lucas's reaction that got the attention of the entire room. The alpha wolf shifter howled and shifted from a man into his wolf form in the blink of an eye. He leapt over the monsters he was fighting and headed for Marie.

Marie's eyes widened and I saw fear in them before she

smirked and said something in Creole before she waved her arms around her body. Shadows broke free from the floor to coalesce around her and her daughter. "Protect your loyal servant," Marie shouted.

The shadows went from translucent to solid smoke. It obscured the two Laveau women hidden inside. I was able to shift my fingers to talons and free myself from the ropes, without adding another cut. Phi helped me with my ankles, and I practically fell into her when I tried to get off the table. My back ached and I stood there like the Hunchback of Notre Dame for a second too long.

Phi helped me hobble to the table two feet from mine where Dre was untying Dahlia's ropes. My breath hitched when I saw the tears shinning in Dre's eyes. "Is she..." I couldn't bring myself to ask the rest of the question.

Dre's head was moving from side to side when her eyes widened and she lunged in our direction. My reaction time was working at a snail's pace while Phi had already engaged the tiny creatures behind us. They were a cross between a small bear and a hyena. They had light brown fur and light blue eyes. The fact that they weren't much taller than a foot should have made them less terrifying, but it didn't. Green slime dripped from their sharp teeth making the stone floor sizzle when it hit. The aura around them was similar to the Dark Fae that looked like a regular person. How two such different creatures could have similar energy signatures was beyond me.

I almost collapsed when I lurched into motion, kicking one of the small Fae creatures. My injuries burned as they broke open while I fought as much as possible. Dre joined us, leaving Lia on the table for the moment. I wanted to grab her and get the hell out of there, but there was no escape at the moment.

Kota and Dea fought their way to us, facing off with more

mambos. Lucas was snapping at the shadows around Marie making faces appear in the smoke. It moved in waves, with what looked like limbs, reaching for the wolf. Noah met my gaze as he shoved a Dark Fae aside. He could have made it to my side, but I could see the debate warring in his eyes.

I motioned to Lucas. "Help him get to Marie." The way Lucas had gone feral told me he was teetering on the brink. I didn't entirely understand what it meant to be fated to a shifter. However, I could tell the pack would lose Lucas if he wasn't able to do something to vent the uncontrolled rage that had come over him hearing about Lia's attack.

Marie had been stupid to underestimate what the shifters would do for us. They would always come to our rescue. Everyone in the pack would lay their lives on the line for us because we were mates to their leaders.

Magic of some kind broke through my racing thoughts and knocked me back into Lia's table. It wasn't Marie or her daughter. Balancing myself on the side of the platform, I scanned the room for anyone focusing on me. Kota and Dea were now helping Dre and Phi with the tiny beasts.

The mambos had stopped chanting as shifters engaged them. The room wasn't very big, and it was crammed with bodies. I tried to focus and send air currents to push the mambos back away from the shifters. When that didn't work, I tried a spell. I had no energy to power the enchantment, so I wasn't surprised when it didn't work. A cry from behind me made me turn around.

My sisters were becoming overwhelmed with the tiny Dark Fae monsters, so I rejoined them, catching one of the bear-hyena creatures before it landed on Kota's back. I tossed it to the side and continued fighting the things. A loud shriek made everything stop a second later.

Turning to the side, I watched as the shadows around Marie disappeared. Several things happened at once just then. Marie's daughter stabbed the bear-hyena I'd tossed away. Somehow it had cut through whatever spell was protecting them. Lucas jumped at the Voodoo Queen and closed his mouth around her throat while Noah punched a mambo sending her sailing through the air.

Lucas jerked his head back, ripping Marie Laveau's throat out. What seemed like a never-ending battle stopped suddenly when Marie's daughter screamed and sent Lucas flying backward. The mambos raced away from the shifters they'd been fighting to snatch up their Queen.

Noah tried to attack but the Dark Fae renewed theirs. My sisters and I couldn't move from our spot. The creatures we were fighting were like cockroaches, hard to kill and coming out of the woodwork in droves. I stomped on them, kicked them and used my witch fire on them. The problem was I didn't have enough energy to maintain control and had to put the flames out before they spread and killed us all. None of us resorted to killing everyone given the situation.

We fought for what seemed like an hour, until the Dark Fae started retreating. Lucas stopped fighting and headed to Lia. He stopped short and howled when he came across a dead shifter. I crouched by him and put my fingers in his fur. "Lia needs you. She could die on us. I'm not sure my spell will hold her for long."

Lucas lifted a bloody muzzle to me and nodded. My legs gave out when I tried to stand and I fell to my ass. Noah knelt next to me and helped me to my feet. "I've got you, Sunshine." I scanned the room and noted that the shifters and my sisters were the only other ones in the place. All of our enemies had fled or been killed.

I let him help me. "I knew you'd come no matter what Marie said. The gargoyle was a surprise."

Noah brought me closer. "We will always come. The witches are outside keeping Marie's wards at bay. They were made using Blood Magic and took more than expected to break through. Let's get out of here."

I turned to Dre. "Call Kip and ask her to meet us at Willowberry. Lia will need her."

Dre took out her phone and typed out a message while Noah helped me through the door. We entered a dark tunnel that seemed to go on forever. It was difficult to keep up as I walked beside Noah. At the end of the tunnel, we didn't reach the end.

I was sucking in air while we walked through endless passages. One of my sisters had conjured a light at some point so we weren't traveling in complete darkness. We encountered a few rooms that looked like they'd been carved out of rock but no one was inside. When I felt a tug on my core, I realized I was still feeding the spell to reach my family. Now that it wasn't needed, I cut it off.

My body shuddered as I tried to remain on my feet as we made our way through the underground tunnels. My legs gave out on me and Noah scooped me up into his arms. I wanted to curl into his body heat and close my eyes, but I couldn't. I was terrified that if I took them off of Dahlia that she would die on us.

It was a miracle that she was alive at all. That knife had slammed right over where her heart should have been. I wanted to believe that my spell protected her from being killed instantly. I'd wondered before if our mom or Leo or some other guardian angel was looking out for us with all the serious shit that we'd escaped. Now I was certain we had someone protecting us from the spirit realm. Nothing else made sense.

Heat and humidity engulfed us the second we left the underground tunnels. We hadn't come across Marie's daughter, her mambos, or Marie herself. I wondered if she survived Lucas's attack. I hoped she died in agony after what she'd done to Lia and me. If that made me a monster, so be it. I wasn't feeling very forgiving at the moment. Lia's life was hanging in the balance. Not to mention that Marie had spent her life manipulating and using others. She killed without thought and planned horrific things for the entire planet by letting Samedi loose.

When anger and a need for vengeance surged within me, I had to rethink my callous attitude toward Marie's fate. I spent my life helping others. As a NICU nurse, I had worked with the most vulnerable, premature babies fighting to stay alive. This malicious darkness that had entered my heart wasn't me. It was almost as if one of Marie's spells was finally taking hold. The thought scared the shit out of me. I fought against it. I didn't want to be like Marie.

My battle with anger was momentarily forgotten when I caught sight of our surroundings. We were in the middle of the bayou somewhere. I was certain we'd been held beneath the Laveau family tomb. Marie had all but confirmed that suspicion when she talked about the power of her ancestors boosting her protections. How the hell had she gotten us out this far? I didn't recall passing through a portal. Although, as we were escaping, we never encountered the living area I'd seen when we were taken.

Regardless of how we got here, we were in the middle of a swamp and Dahlia didn't have much time. I prayed to our guardian angel to keep looking out for her as Lucas led the way home with Lia in his arms.

CHAPTER 7

DAHLIA

My chest felt like an elephant was sitting on top of it. The weight was oppressive and made breathing feel like I was sucking in fumes from the fires of hell. What was happening to me? This wasn't quite as bad as when I was attacked by the skin walker, but just as disorienting. While wracking my brain for what had happened, images surfaced of Marie Laveau torturing us while her mambos and tall, lithe, stunning Dark Fae watched with growing excitement. The Queen of Voodoo had plunged a knife into my chest.

I almost wondered if I was dead when the ache made the question moot. There was no way I'd be in any pain if I wasn't alive. I couldn't hear anything aside from my thundering heartbeat in my ears. A sharp spike in pain made me suck in a breath. It was the bouncing of my body that caused the discomfort. I braced myself for impact, hoping I wasn't being tossed about. The last thing I recalled was Lucas and a massive stone gargoyle busting into the room where Dani and I were being held.

My heart raced and I tried to open my eyes as my fear for Dani dumped adrenaline into my system. The sight above me made me feel so many things at once. Relief, joy, and hope. Lucas held me and based on the way the sky above my head bounced around, he'd rescued me.

"Shhh, Flower. I've got you," Lucas reassured me.

I sagged against him. "Dani?" My voice was a dry croak as I spoke. I had the worst case of cotton mouth ever known to man.

"She's going to be fine. So are you. We're getting you to Kip," Lucas promised.

"Lia!" My name was called out by numerous people at once. All of them familiar. Several heads popped around Lucas's shoulder as his movements slowed slightly. My sisters looked haggard and happy at the same time. Dani was the only one that didn't look me over. I turned my head to see her cradled in Noah's arms.

"Thank god you're alive," Dre said as she squeezed my foot.

Dakota nodded, wiping her brow with the back of her hand. "Shitballs, Lia, you get into more shit than anyone I know."

One corner of my mouth lifted. "It's because I can handle it. At least that's what mama used to say. I'm not so sure I agree." The last several words came out more of a breathless whisper. I didn't have the oxygen.

"Don't talk right now, love. Save your energy." Lucas's mouth pursed and his eyes were haunted as he looked down at me.

Looking down, I saw the hole in my chest. "How had that knife missed my heart? It should have cut through the middle of it." I closed my eyes as dizziness washed over me making the world spin.

"I cast a spell when I saw Marie with the knife," Dani said. "I wasn't sure it would work."

My eyes shot open and met Dani's fatigued brown ones. Adrenalin giving me a temporary boost. "That's because you're a badass witch."

Dani snorted. "You mean I'm a badass mutt. We're more than simple witches." She flicked one of her fingers up making it shift into a talon as it rose.

Movement behind her distracted me. "Over there." It felt like my arm weighed a hundred pounds to lift it an inch and point to where I'd seen something move.

Lucas stopped instantly along with the rest of our group. He and Noah went on alert at the same time dozens of people swarmed around us. I lifted my head and would have pushed at Lucas to put me down, but I could hardly breathe, let alone move very much. We needed to get out of here. That thought brought me up short as I realized I had no idea where the hell we were.

The absence of buildings and presence of Spanish moss-covered cypress trees told me we were in the bayou. I thought we were at St. Louis Cemetery Number One based on the bones we'd encountered while digging, the claim by Marie that her ancestors were adding strength to her wards and the fact that the Laveau family tomb was located there.

Normally, I was annoyed with myself when I was wrong about something. In this situation I was downright pissed. We were in the bayou somewhere. Nothing looked familiar. We were far from help. My head dropped back, and I noticed the witches behind the shifters, surrounding us. Kaitlyn was there, along with several other people I recognized. I moved my eyes to the head witch who raced to my side.

"We need to stop meeting like this," Kaitlyn told me as

Lucas laid me on the ground. "I boosted Dani's spell to keep your wound from getting worse. Don't worry, we will get you to Kip in time."

I swallowed, trying not to choke on my thick saliva. "I'm not so sure." My chest burned and the pressure increased to near excruciating levels. It was all I could do not to pass out, or throw up. And it took all of my effort to keep from crying out.

Noah set Dani next to me. Kota went to her knees next to me, with Dre next to Dani, and Phi and Dea in front of us. Kota wrapped an arm around my shoulders and pulled me into her side. "Shut the hell up, sestra. You're the positive one. I'm the one that's supposed to be whining about the bullshit we're in this time."

I lifted one corner of my mouth as I watched the shifters close ranks around the seven of us. Kaitlyn remained next to my sisters and I while Lucas and Noah shifted into their wolves then took off running.

Dani leaned into Phi for support. "Why are we out here?"

Kaitlyn lifted up as she watched the direction where Lucas and Noah had disappeared. "Because Laveau moved the bulk of her operations from her place under St Louis Cemetery Number One to the bayou after Phoebe paid her a visit. Never piss off a god of any kind. Especially not one from the Underworld. Aidon threatened to destroy Marie's wards if she ever cut him off from his mate again."

Marie might have been working on the location, but she couldn't have had it all that long or she would have moved her mambos out there when she was trying to sacrifice a mundie to serve as host for Samedi. My guess was that the Dark Fae helped her create the underground facility. I felt the magic as we moved through the space and not all of it was Marie's.

"Noah believes she did it to make it harder for shifters to

find her. With all the animals and other smells of the bayou, it's harder for a shifter to pick up a single scent." A guy in front of us added. It was Jeremy, the guy that mated Lucas's daughter Lily.

"I don't doubt that's true," Dani replied. "She said no one was going to risk coming for us. How long have we been gone? It feels like it has been forever."

"Two damn days," Dea said. "We've been scrying every minute until a couple of hours ago when we finally got a lock on your location. The good news is that I can find those jeans I lost in high school now."

Kota inclined her head. "Yeah, we're now experts in scrying."

I smiled at Kota. "That's why you found us."

Dre's forehead furrowed. "How come your signal appeared a few hours ago? It had been hidden completely. How did you get through?"

Dani lifted her mud-covered hands and bloody fingertips. "It was only after we finally managed to dig below Marie's spells that we were able to send out a signal. We encountered bones, which made us believe we were under her family tomb."

Kaitlyn's mouth dropped open. "That's why we got a signal in the cemetery first. It moved to the bayou so fast I assumed it was a trick of Marie's magic."

I shook my head, trying to think straight. "How did she move us so far? It felt like moving from one room to another. It didn't take that long."

Kaitlyn shrugged her shoulders. "The only explanation is magic. I didn't think Marie could create portals. It's possible that the loa was here long enough to create one for her."

"How long was it before you knew we were missing, anyway?" Dani asked. We hadn't given them a time frame for our absence, so it could have taken them awhile. Everyone was busy with their own lives, not keeping track of where we were.

Dea rubbed a hand over her heart. "I felt your fear. I was on the floor giving a patient some pain killers and I almost dropped to my knees it was so intense. I excused myself and called your cell phones. When you didn't answer, I dialed Dre. She and Kota left to look for you immediately."

Dre rubbed her shoulders. "We saw your car the second we arrived at the craft store. When we didn't find you inside, we asked the clerks if they had seen you. Kota nearly throttled the cashier when she refused to give us your purses and purchases."

"That bitch called the cops and said she was going to hand it over to them. We had to go home and get your spare key so we could drive your car home." Kota shook with anger next to me as she recounted the experience. "We got lucky that we showed up before the police. Lucas handled the officers when they arrived. We had no idea what to say to them. He let them take your purses and purchases. We're going to have to pick up everything when you're better."

Dani scowled as she listened. "I'm surprised no one stole the car. I was certain it would be in a chop shop somewhere."

"Mama was looking over you guys," Dre replied. "Some woman closed your trunk and brought your stuff inside the store, telling the employees she found it on the ground and was concerned that something had happened to you."

Kota let out a tiny shriek after a growl shook the ground beneath us. My eyes flew open and I grabbed Kota's side. Our sisters and Kaitlin moved closer to me and Dani, surrounding us with their protection. The shifters crouched in front of us, their noses twitching like crazy. I held my breath as we waited for something to happen. My nerves were strung tight, and my body was shaky, from the constant adrenaline rushes combined with the injury.

Kaitlyn shook her head. "Lucas and Noah found something, or someone, but I can't get a lock on what."

"It's probably Dark Fae. They're Marie's new best friends," I replied.

Kaitlyn's quizzical expression landed on me. "Dark Fae? How did she manage that? Phoebe promised her friend wouldn't let them through the portal."

"The magical disturbance during the Second Line Parade opened a temporary portal and Marie brought them through." I shuddered as I recalled the glee in Marie's eyes when she told us about how we'd been instrumental in allowing another evil into our realm.

I saw two wolves leap through the air and pounce on some animals. From this distance they looked like bears, but they were way too small for that to be the case. Not to mention bears didn't live in the bayou.

"What were those things?" Dani pointed to the bloody mess Lucas and Noah were making of the creatures. "They looked like bear-hyena hybrids."

"If you're right and Marie is working with the Dark Fae, those might be *mausles*. I've only read about them in books. I couldn't identify them earlier because I was thinking of beings native to the area, and voodoo in particular," Kaitlyn explained. "They're blood thirsty and difficult to kill but not terribly intelligent."

Dani shuddered as Lucas and Noah attacked several more that rushed through the ground cover. "They remind me of cockroaches."

My heart tried to race when a dozen, or more, made it past Lucas and Noah then headed right for us. Was Marie controlling them? They seemed to have their sights set on our group. The shifters shot into motion, intercepting them before they managed to breach their defensive circle around us.

Wind picked up, blowing my hair around my face and making it hard to keep my eyes on the action. When Dre was blown backward, I knew one of the human-looking Fae had to be close. "There have to be Dark Fae nearby."

Lucas's head lifted, and his gaze locked onto me when I said that. Ignoring the *mausles*, he raced from the trees. His wolf form sailed through the air when a fierce gust hit his side. He shot right up and continued on his path toward me.

Kaitlyn grabbed Kota's hand. "Cast a spell of protection around us, now. We need to make sure we can't be touched so the shifters can deal with this threat."

I was of no help, but I felt when my sisters and the witches cast the ward around our group. Lucas changed course and went to the left. It was then that I noticed the group of Dark Fae hiding behind trees. They dropped their hands and took off running with Lucas, Noah, and a handful of other shifters in pursuit.

My shoulders tightened along with my gut as I watched the shifters fight the *mausles*. Blood bits flew around the swamp, some splashing when they hit water while others splatted as they hit the dirt. Worry made my breathing even choppier as I moved my focus to the area where Lucas had taken off after the Dark Fae. There were no sounds to tell me what was happening. The shifters closest to us had finally taken care of all the small bear-hyena creatures and didn't seem concerned.

The band around my chest loosened significantly when Lucas walked out of the woods in his human form. He moved through the throng of shifters that had surrounded us. My cheeks heated when he bent in all his glory and picked me up. Dre clapped me on the shoulder lightly with a chuckle. "You and Dani need to start carrying clothes for your mates. Normally, I wouldn't mind seeing such naked perfection but since he's basically a brother-in-law to us now, it's not so comfortable."

"Next time, I'll be sure," I replied then took a break to catch my breath. The blood loss and kidnapping were taking their toll. This latest delay had made things worse for me. "To tell my kidnappers to let me grab the go bag in my car."

Lucas pressed his lips to the top of my head. "My pack has clothes for me, but we need to get you to Kip, who is waiting for us at Willowberry."

The snickers from my sisters stopped immediately making Lucas's words carry even more weight. I knew I was in bad shape. I shouldn't even be alive. The blow would have killed me if Dani hadn't saved my life. She was the reason I was able to even think at the moment. If not for her spell, I would not be coherent right now.

It took many years for me to see my siblings as the blessing they truly are in my life. Growing up wearing hand-me-downs and not having water or electricity wasn't easy but we managed. Now, I wouldn't trade them for the world. It was reassuring going through all this paranormal chaos with five of the fiercest bitches I knew at my back.

I was beyond wishing our new lives were simpler with less danger. Being injured was becoming old hat by now and I wasn't about to let this incident make me back down. Marie wouldn't stop if we let up now. Yes, I was counting on her survival. The injury would have killed a mundie but that's not what we were dealing with. And her followers had shown they were willing to sacrifice everything to ensure her survival.

"After I'm healed, we need to find Marie," I said in a ragged voice.

Lucas lifted one brow and his stormy grey eyes looked into mine. "Let's table that for a later discussion. She won't be rebuilding anywhere in the swamps. I've contacted the gator shifter alpha to coordinate patrols of the swamps and bayou. Right now, we are focusing on you."

I dipped my head in agreement, relieved that the available space for Marie was shrinking rather than growing. I burrowed into his warmth and listened to his steady heartbeat. It was the opposite of the erratic thumping in my chest. I gasped when he shifted me to one arm so he could open the door to his truck.

Before he could take off a car screeched to a halt and Kip jumped out of the passenger seat. "I knew we shouldn't wait for you to arrive at the plantation. You guys get into more trouble than anyone I know. Set her down, so I can heal her."

Lucas was gentle as he set me down and backed away so the healer could approach. Kip handed me a potion to drink and placed one hand over my wound. She hummed as her healing magic went to work. I tipped the vial back and swallowed the bitter liquid. Warmth filled my body as the cells knitted back together.

"You did great work with that spell, Dani. This injury would have been so much worse." Kip's expression told me I would have died. I owed my sister my life.

Dani's cheeks turned pink. "I didn't stop and think about it. I followed my gut."

"I owe you my life, Dani. I'm so glad you're so brilliant." The pressure in my chest lightened as my wound sealed from the inside out. My lung filled for the first time since I was stabbed clearing some of the haze in my mind. While I felt better, I wasn't one hundred percent. It was like there was a dense fog inside me.

Kip staggered after several seconds and her warmth cut off. She turned, grabbed two jars of paste, and handed one to Noah. "Put this on Dani's cuts. It'll cancel the voodoo magic pumping through her veins."

Dani gasped, her hand flying to her chest. "I felt Marie's

magic enter me. She assumed she could get to me after Lia was mortally wounded."

Kaitlyn cocked her head to the side and looked between Dani and me. "Can you explain that? Specifically, how you managed to evade possession. I warned Lucas and Noah you were likely hosts for some powerful loa."

Kip smeared the paste on my cuts and immediately it felt like a million ants were crawling under my skin. While Kip worked on our wounds, Dani explained how we joined our magic and cast the protection around us. Kaitlyn was shocked it was something Marie couldn't get past. Apparently, in the past nothing had stopped the Queen of Voodoo. It was how she was able to force the necromancers and vampires under her control.

Lucas approached the open door. I was glad to see he had a pair of sweats on along with a t-shirt. "We can discuss the rest of this at the plantation. We need to get out of here before the Dark Fae regroup and come after us."

Everyone separated and piled into the various vehicles. I laid my head against the back of the seat as Lucas pulled out onto the road. I was exhausted but couldn't sleep quite yet. My mind worked through how we could locate Marie before she built another stronghold right under our noses.

CHAPTER 8

DANIELLE

*D*ahlia smirked at me, easing the tension that had been compressing my lungs for the past twenty hours since we were rescued from Marie Laveau's blade. "Go, let Noah cook you dinner. Lucas is here with me if Marie finds a way to get any of her minions past our wards. You need a break from all this paranormal craziness so we can get back to planning that anniversary party."

I sighed and picked up my purse. We all needed a break from the current chaos of our lives. Being able to forget the danger, and near-death experiences, we seemed to encounter every other month was the one thing that kept me sane. Without it, I would have run from the plantation screaming. "Call us if anything happens. The other shoe is going to drop, it's just a matter if time."

Lia lifted a shoulder. I didn't understand how she could be so nonchalant about what had happened to us. She bounced back like a racquet ball without missing a beat. I envied that about her. "I know, and we will respond when it happens. We can't predict what she will do, and sitting around trying to figure it out is only going to drive us to the edge. We need to replenish ourselves so we are in better shape to face her next move."

Lucas cocked his head to the side as he chewed a grape. "She might not have survived my bite, you know."

Lia patted his chest and smiled up at her mate. "Even if that's the case, her daughter will come after us. And she will have even more reason to hate us. I don't think we will be dealing with the next generation Marie just yet, though. The Dark Fae are more powerful than you realize. I felt it when Marie was performing her ritual. And she has her mambos. They're ready to sacrifice anything for their Queen. But all of those concerns can wait. Have fun, Dani. We will be here if you need us."

I chuckled at how well Lia handled Lucas, then waved, as Noah led me to his truck. A shiver traveled down my spine as he leaned close to my ear. "I can bring you back here, if you feel the need, at any time tonight. But I hope you can relax and enjoy some time with me. After two days of searching for you, I need some time just for us."

I smiled at him as he opened the car door. He was hurrying to the driver's side before I could respond. I enjoyed the way his jeans hugged his ass as he climbed behind the wheel. The roar of the engine kept my mind from wandering down a far naughtier path.

Clearing my throat, I buckled up as he pulled out of the lot. "I don't want to come home tonight. It'll be nice to get away from the paranormal world for a bit."

Noah looked over and laughed. "Escaping the paranormal isn't going to happen, love. I'm a shifter and I live in the middle of pack lands."

Swatting his shoulder, I couldn't keep from giggling at his

teasing. "I'm some mixture of several magical creatures, so I know there's no getting away from it. But life at the plantation is more dangerous than skydiving. It's that peril I want to be taken away from."

Noah's mirth faded and was replaced by a smoldering look. "I'll always be your safe haven. All you have to do is say, 'Noah, take me away.'"

Amusement bubbled up as I thought of that commercial from my childhood about a woman escaping in a bubble bath and shared those thoughts. Noah's humor returned and he was once again laughing. "I remember those commercials and their ridiculous claims."

I pursed my lips to hid my smile. "I don't know about that. Never underestimate the power of a good soak. It works miracles on a body."

"I know something else that will relax and enliven you at the same time." Noah's tone was husky and more than hinted where his thoughts had gone. This combination of sexual tension, laughter, and camaraderie was refreshing. In my experience, men were equipped to handle one emotion at a time. And the second anything remotely sexual came up they tended to get stuck on that topic and keeping the conversation in that direction.

We passed the short drive to Noah's house bantering back and forth like that. It was a nice break from topics that carried the weight of the world. I felt fifty pounds lighter by the time he pulled up in front of his place. If only it was actual weight, I would be in great shape. Turning forty had done a number on my metabolism and it was only going to get worse as time passed.

Noah was at my door and helping me down before I managed to get the panel opened. I waved to several shifters who were wandering around the area, then followed Noah inside. The smell of garlic and fried chicken greeted me. "Mmmm, it smells heavenly in here."

Noah's cheeks pinkened as he shifted his focus to the oven in his kitchen. "I made your favorites. They might be a little soggy by now though."

I joined him as he opened the oven. This close, I was able to see it was set to warm. "You made fried green tomatoes, too? You can't go wrong with this meal."

Noah beamed at me as he pulled the pans out and set them on top of the stove before he grabbed a bowl from the fridge. "The remoulade is an old family recipe. It's a little different, so I hope you like it."

I dipped a finger in the sauce and popped in in my mouth. An appreciative hum rumbled up my throat. "That is delicious. I'll need to test it with some fried green tomato to be sure."

A smile spread over my face as I cut a piece and dipped it in the sauce. I groaned as I chewed the crispy, spicy vegetable. "I need this recipe. Not that I cook much, but Kota and Dre do, and they'd love this. Do you enjoy putting together meals?"

Noah picked up a tomato and dunked it in the dip. "I've never minded it but suddenly, it's my favorite thing in the world. Providing for you fulfills me, but seeing you enjoy this so much makes it all the better. Tell me more of your favorites."

I considered how to explain this as I picked up a piece of chicken. "I have a few favorites that I tend to eat often like bean burritos and chicken. I like several different kinds of food and am open to trying new things, especially if you make them. Just know that most of what I try I don't like."

Noah picked up a piece of tomato dipped in sauce and held it to my mouth. The chicken in my hand was forgotten as I opened my mouth and leaned forward so Noah could feed me. "I consider that a challenge. And I'll be sure to have backups in case you don't care for what I've made."

My heart melted over how willing he was to accommodate my tastes rather than making me feel bad. "I'm a hard woman to please."

Noah closed the distance between us and ran a finger down the side of my neck. My body reacted to his touch immediately. Pleasure coursed through my veins, and I leaned into him for more. It was crazy how such a light caress signaled my body that it was time to get ready for more.

Noah's mouth pressed the outer shell of my ear, his hot breath tickling me. "You seem to respond very well to me. I think I need to tease you some more to be sure you're getting enough pleasure."

Turning, I lifted my hands to his shoulders and ran them over his smooth muscles. "If anyone can rise to the occasion, it's you. After all, your skill is legendary."

I squealed when Noah lifted me up and carried me to his living room. "Ignore anything other women have said. I didn't truly come to life until I met you. I lived my life half asleep before I saw you the very first time."

Warmth and affection filled me to bursting. It shoved aside the horrendous experience of being kidnapped and held by Laveau. I forced the mental voice in my head aside to keep it from making fun of the mushy exclamation. Typically, I would gag or stick my finger down my throat if a guy said something like this to me. It made me uncomfortable, because I usually sensed his ulterior motive beneath his words and that removed any meaning from what was said. Noah wasn't angling to get into my pants or get a motorcycle, or something like that. He was telling me his truth and I would always honor that.

Wrapping my arms around his neck, I smiled. "Don't

worry. I've never talked with one of your ex-girlfriends. I'm speaking from experience."

Noah set me on the couch and knelt in front of me. He cupped my cheeks. The heat in his green eyes felt like it was enough to burn away every scrap of clothing I was wearing. My body tingled and arousal coated my panties. He pressed his lips to mine. "I want to feast on you, but not if you want to eat first."

I ran a hand down his chest and gripped his cock through the fabric of his jeans making him suck in a breath. "I'd rather have dessert first. I have a sudden craving for...caramel." I chewed on my lower lip as I looked at him through hooded lids.

"Mmmm, I have a bottle of milk caramel that I think you'll like."

He jumped up and raced to the fridge making my hand fall away from his groin. He was back in a flash with a plastic bottle. I reached down and lifted my shirt over my head. "I'm going to need your clothes off to taste test that stuff." I lifted my ass and unzipped my pants then shoved them down over my legs.

My mouth watered at the sight of his chest muscles rippling as he moved. He had the most perfect body ever created. He earned every hill and valley through hard work. I was a lucky woman to get someone like him. I was fifteen pounds overweight and carried it in the worst place, my stomach. It hadn't been flat since I had my twins almost twenty years ago.

"What if I want to test it out first? Your nipples are pert and begging for some attention. Lay back and take off the rest." Noah's voice was husky as he kicked his shoes off.

When Noah popped the button of his jeans, his cock jumped beneath the cotton of his boxer briefs. An ache to be

FRENCH QUARTER FAE

filled by him made me unbutton my bra and toss it aside before removing my panties.

I shook my head from side to side. "I'm calling the shots today," I said with a seductive smile.

His eyes widened when I slid his boxer briefs to the floor. His body went rigid as he kicked the fabric to the side. He shuddered when I ran a hand down the side of his thigh. His shaft hardened and lengthened as I stared at him.

His reaction to me gave me courage. "Have a seat," I instructed and patted the cushion next to me.

I could see the curiosity brimming in his eyes. I went to my knees in front of him as he sat down. He smiled at me and reached for my waist. I swatted his hand away. "Nope. No touching unless I give you permission. It's my turn."

Noah groaned. "Damn, I love this aggressive side of you. My wolf is howling in agreement. Whay have you been hiding this side of yourself?"

I picked up the plastic bottle from the end table and flipped it open. I shifted one hand to talons and ran one of them up the inside of his thigh. "I've never hidden anything from you, Dimples. I'm not the same woman I was four months ago. I'm a brand-new person with exciting cravings."

"You can have anything you want. All you have to do is ask." His promise came out in a strained voice.

A smile lifted the corners of my mouth before I upended the bottle. Keeping my gaze locked with his, I squeezed a thin stream of the caramel on the tip of his cock. Drops hit his stomach when his shaft jerked as the cool liquid hit his flesh. My mouth watered for an entirely different reason. The sweet, buttery, vanilla scent mixed with Noah's masculine aroma to create a delicious treat.

"You're driving me crazy," he croaked making me lift my head.

"I can see precisely how much you like it." I lowered my

head and claimed his lips in a passionate kiss. His tongue licked along my mouth seeking entrance. I denied him and moved my mouth across his cheek then down his neck.

I recalled my talons and slid my warm hands up his thighs, then broke the kiss. My hand reached the juncture of his thighs, then I bent over his lap and ran my tongue up the underside of his cock where the dessert sauce had dripped. It was sweet and salty at the same time.

One hand went to his chest and ran up it. I lifted my eyes and saw the strain on his face. He was clenching his hands at his sides, fighting the urge to grab me by the hair and shove his erection into my mouth. I don't know how he held back. I never did when he licked my clit and gave me oral pleasure.

Noah's heat increased as his shaft got harder. Lifting higher on my knees, I licked all around making sure to clean every scrap of caramel from his cock. I closed my mouth around his shaft. His girth pushed my jaw to its limit, but I didn't stop sucking him to the back of my throat. I choked when he went too far. Pulling back, I sucked the head into my mouth and ran my tongue over the spongey tip.

Next, I wrapped my hand around him and squeezed. His arousal coated my tongue as his moans increased. His hands landed on my shoulders and ran down my back before he reached around and grabbed a breast. I moaned making his cock vibrate in my mouth. His hips jerked, shoving more of his erection into my mouth. I closed my lips around him and was pulled off a second later.

I flew through the air when he lifted me off the ground. His cock was pulled from my mouth, and he settled me on the couch next to him a second later. One hand went between my soft breasts. His other hand suddenly grabbed my jaw and tilted my head. His mouth crashed against mine. His kiss was rough and desperate. I groaned when his tongue forced my lips apart. He delved inside, stroking his tongue against mine with determination. Noah's hot breath caressed my face as he explored my mouth.

"I need to touch you," Noah murmured against my mouth. His words were hesitant making me wonder if he doubted my affection. Replaying what he said a couple minutes ago, I realized he was likely reluctant because he didn't want to interrupt my fun.

His lips left mine and he went to the floor this time. His green eyes held mine as he reached up, latching onto my breasts. He squeezed the lush globes, his grin growing when I moaned long and loud. "Noah." I wasn't sure if I was telling him to stop so I could resume what I was doing, or telling him to not stop. All I knew is that I arched into his grip.

His thumbs found my turgid peaks. I cried out as he pulled and twisted until my nipples lengthened and hardened. Noah leaned forward for a bite. I gently pushed his head back and grabbed his hands. "Not yet," I whispered. Holy crap, my willpower was slipping. All I could hear was my heavy breathing and erratic heartbeat. It got worse the more turned on I got.

Noah kissed a path up my chest and the side of my neck. I wrapped my fingers around him and stroked him from base to tip several times. His arousal leaked making it easier for my hand to glide over his flesh like a well-oiled machine. I massaged and caressed freely. Noah widened his knees to grant me more access.

"Dani," he panted.

I pushed his chest back with my free hand. With his back straight and me still sitting on the couch, I bent over and kissed along his shaft. Hearing the sounds that he made as I pleasured him turned me on and made me wet as hell. I understood why he enjoyed doing that to me so often.

"Ah, fuck," he groaned when I sucked him to the back of my throat. His head fell back, and his hands braced his weight on the cushion next to my legs. I groaned when they pressed against my overheated flesh.

The sweet sounds of licking and sucking filled the room. I pushed him closer to the edge of climax. His cock twitched, and his balls tightened with his building release as I lightly tickled the space behind his ball-sack.

"I won't last long, Dani." His words came out clipped.

"Hmmm," I hummed against his shaft. "You have a problem with that?"

"Fuck it. I've got this now." His words were a growl as he scooped me in his arms then set me on the floor. He grabbed a blanket and spread it out on top of the rug.

"I wasn't done." I squealed as he prowled between my legs.

"You are now," he countered and dipped his head. "I'm hungry, too."

I watched as Noah's tongue swiped through my feminine folds. I was so much weaker than he was. My back arched and my legs wrapped around his shoulders as he feasted on my sex. The one thing I noticed about him was that his tongue was much rougher than normal. I attributed it to his shifter status. Whatever the reason, I couldn't get enough. I wasn't kidding when I told Noah that he was legendary. He was a master of oral sex.

He inserted a finger inside my body making me grab his head. I was wanton as I pressed myself against his mouth. As pleasure took over my body, I hoped that I gave him a fraction of the pleasure he provided me. This was Heaven on Earth. His tongue swirled across my clit in such a delicious way.

"Don't stop." It wasn't necessary to beg. Noah had proven to me already that he would never leave me hanging. I got a jolt to my system when I realized that I trusted him. I'd never felt closer to someone than I did Noah.

His loud moan made me buck wildly. He was relentless in

his torture, and I was his willing victim. I groaned when he paused. I looked down with a frown as my chest rose and fell rapidly. His sexy smirk made my heart beat faster.

"So fucking perfect," he murmured as he licked his lips.

This man was meant for me. It was the only explanation for the ease of our relationship. Talking to Noah was easy and comfortable. I was never uncomfortable around him. And the best part was how amazing the sex was. The pain I experienced with previous partners was completely gone. I loved this man with my whole heart. I especially loved what his finger was doing inside me at that moment.

"You were perfect until you stopped that magic tongue of yours." I yelped when he ran his tongue through my slit before he sucked on my clit.

There was more pressure as another finger slid through my channel and into my body. My muscles clenched around the digits. He continued licking my clit and pumping his fingers in and out of me. It didn't take long before I shouted my release then rode the tidal wave of ecstasy. Stars exploded in my vision. I grabbed hold of his shoulders, clinging to him like he was a lifeline.

"Noah." The climax left me aching for more only I couldn't formulate words with the pleasure turning my brain to mush.

He chuckled and lifted his head. "Ready for more?"

I nodded as my chest heaved and I caught my breath. He prowled up my body, spreading my legs with his muscular frame. He grabbed my hands and held them above my head as he positioned his cock at my entrance. I wrapped my legs around his waist and locked my ankles behind his back, pulling him to my center.

He leaned down and claimed my lips. "I need you inside me, now." I spoke against his mouth. He lifted his torso and met my gaze. Bright green pools of desire mirrored what I felt.

"You never have to ask twice," he countered then thrust inside my body with one hard stroke.

My gasp was closer to a scream as Noah stretched and filled me. He slowly pulled out then shoved deeper. I rocked my hips, seeking that spot that sent me over the edge. I was still wound tight despite the release. I had needed his cock. He had me addicted to him. No man ever came close to my G-spot, but Noah owned it. Length, girth, and stamina. The man had it all.

"More," I growled and bucked against his body.

Noah climbed to his knees and grabbed my hips. "Fuck, I want you so bad. My need is out of control. Stop me if it gets too rough." He panted and started to move in and out of my body with a force I hadn't seen before. It bordered on painful but didn't cross to the point that I had to ask him to stop. It heightened every sensation.

Lifting my head, I pressed my lips to his chest and kissed a path to his nipples. I caressed his sides and down. When my hands encountered his muscular ass, I couldn't stop myself from grabbing hold. I licked and sucked his nipples making his cock grow and harden inside me. My muscles clenched as I got closer to another climax.

His eyes locked with mine as he plundered me. It didn't take long before we reached our peak together. Our bond flared in my chest, heating me and adding to my pleasure.

I dropped my head and sighed at the same time he dropped to his side next to me. "I love you, Sunshine."

The corners of my mouth lifted as joy spread through me and combined with my contentment. "I love you, too. Now that we've had dessert, I think it's time for dinner. We've got to restore our energy so we can go again."

Noah pressed his lips to mine then popped up, grabbed a

tray, then added the dishes to it before grabbing a couple of forks and a tall boy and a beer from the fridge. I watched wondering how his cock was still hard as a rock. That man had the stamina of ten teenaged boys. Not that I was complaining.

I grabbed Noah's t-shirt and sat cross legged. He opened my drink and handed me a chicken leg. I nibbled on some food while Noah ate several pieces of chicken. The potatoes were flavorful and creamy. We laughed and ate while talking about the anniversary party. He told me a little more about Lincoln and Gracie, Stasia's parents. The more food I put in my belly, the sleepier I got.

I worried for a second that he would be disappointed if we didn't have sex again. My muscles tightened as I looked at Noah. "I'm tired. How about you?"

Noah ran a hand over my hair before pulling me with him as he laid down. "I could use a nap before I ravish your body again."

Full and happy, I laid my head on Noah's chest. snuggling into his side, then let go of my past. I'd been using my previous failed marriages as a shield. And it had served its purpose. I didn't go into this relationship with Noah blind. Quite the opposite. I had gone out with him but held part of myself back until tonight. It wasn't easy allowing the newness of things with him to take me to that happy place all relationships went in the beginning. That had bitten me on the ass one too many times. That reticence had robbed us of the honeymoon phase. Although, it put us in a more realistic status from the beginning, so there's no fall from this high peak.

My connection with Noah hummed steadily in my chest. It was so different from anything I'd ever experienced before, and it had frightened me initially. It was that bond that gave me the courage to fully trust that Noah and I were in this together for the long haul. Not having the answers to how my life would play out with him made me twitchy as hell. I hated ambiguity. It was my nemesis. And it caused my psychotic mind to shift into high gear now that I'd let go of my past. Now, I was in full planning mode. Like I did with parties, I began envisioning where Noah was going to live and how things would play out between us. *Stop! Go with the flow this time. Not everything needs to be laid out right now.* That was easier said than done. It took several more minutes of me focusing on Noah's even breathing while I told myself to take it one day at a time. As my eyes drifted closed, a smile spread over my lips. The details didn't matter at the moment. It was enough to trust that he loved me and would always be there for me. I'd worry about keeping that frame of mind when I woke up.

CHAPTER 9

DANIELLE

I looked around the greenhouse attached to our magical kitchen lost in my head, bot really invested in the gardening. Lucas and Noah had helped us update one of the smaller buildings at the back of our land to act as the space where we created potions and stored our magical accoutrement so it wasn't seen by the tourists roaming through the main plantation house on a daily basis.

Our kitchen was a spacious one-bedroom bungalow. The kitchen and living room were one open space where we had tables set up with our cauldrons, shelving units with supplies and a full kitchen. The room had a bed and there was the bathroom. The plan was to remodel all of the former slave quarters on the back of the property and rent them out on one of the online short-term rental apps. Noah and Lucas were making progress with the other buildings now that this one was finished.

Dre dropped the trowel she was using. "We need to practice offensive spells, sestras."

Turning away from the open door of the greenhouse where we grew various herbs and plants for our potions, I focused on what Dreya had said. She was the oldest of the Six Twisted Sisters and the most protective. Given what Lia and I had recently gone through at the hands of the Queen of Voodoo, I wasn't surprised by her suggestion. Both of us were still suffering from the aging spell Marie put on us. Kaitlyn wasn't sure how much they could reverse of that curse.

Kota set the watering can down and cocked her head to the side. "Good idea. I'd like to be able to fry Marie's ass if she ever tried to kidnap me. Do you have any ideas for spells to practice?"

Phi gestured to the back door of our magical kitchen. "I've asked Kaitlyn for some spells that we should have in our family grimoire, but we haven't gotten very far. And none of them are offensive. It's been stuff like cleaning spells, creating light balls, and nutrient spells for our greenhouse."

My mind played through what Lia and I accomplished when facing torment and death. "We don't need Kaitlyn. We can create our own."

Lia's eyes widened and she nodded. "Yes! What matters is our intent. Dani and I held Marie off for twenty-four hours. And then we sent a signal to you guys. Kaitlyn taught us basic protection spells but ours went beyond that. We can do this."

Dea threw her hands up as she smiled at us. "Alright then, let's go outside so we don't blow up this nice building. With our luck we might still destroy the trees. We should warn Talewen and the others."

Dre chuckled. "Nah, we'll go to the center of where the

tobacco used to grow. It's far enough away from their mound and there's nothing out there that we can damage."

Kota headed out the door first. "I'm going to try and shift into a dragon. Could you imagine Marie's reaction if she kidnapped us again and she was suddenly facing reptilian creatures capable of eating her?"

Dea started laughing as we headed across our property. "It would be highly satisfying to bite her head off. Although, I'm sure she'd give us a bad case of indigestion."

We stopped when we reached the middle of the field and spread out. Talewen and Jelin flew from their mound to join us. Talewen was the leader of the mound at Willowberry. Both pixies waved at us. "Do you mind if we watch? We overheard you talking and are eager to see how your magic works given your mixed heritage," Talewen said as she hovered close by. Her green hair flew around her shoulders in the wind created by her iridescent wings.

"That would be wonderful. If we get to testing whether or not we can manipulate the elements, we could use your advice," Lia replied.

Phi held up a hand. "We're going to be trying to reach our dragon heritage first. Do you have any advice? I know you said dragon shifters are Fae."

Jelin nodded and moved her hands in a circle around her torso. She wore a pale-yellow dress and had her sapphire hair tied back. "I spent time with the royal family before Teague took the throne. Look for the fire buried within the center of your being. That's where the dragon emerges. I don't know how you can coax it out, though."

I thought about what I felt when I shifted my fingers into talons. My chest definitely filled with heat when that happened. I was confident that I'd be able to find that part of me. I sat down on the grass and crossed my legs. "I usually concentrate on my fingers and think about shifting them into talons."

Lia flexed her fingers in front of her face. "Talons and heat. I can do that."

I watched the rest of my sisters do their own version of a pep talk before they fell silent. I decided to use Jelin's advice and look inward for the heat in my chest. There was gurgling, hunger, and organs being squished by my fifteen pounds of extra weight but no heat. My heart started racing as my panic rose. If I got frustrated, I would lose the ability to shift at all.

I sucked in a breath and resorted to what I'd always done. Focusing on my fingers, I pictured them turning into talons. The heat popped up a second later and I turned my attention there. It seemed as if there was a gas burner set to medium close to my diaphragm. The more I focused on it, the hotter it got.

I pictured my fingers shifting and wings sprouting out of my back while imagining a bellows feeding the fire making it increase. The heat decreased some when Lia cried out saying she managed to shift her hands. I had to shut out my sisters when Kota was next and started talking about getting a manicure on her talons.

Shutting out everything around us, I mentally pumped the bellows and added more details to my dragon. In no time it felt as if I had an inferno going in my chest. It was surprisingly not painful at all. It never hurt to change my fingers. My muscles flexed and moved as if I was doing yoga.

I allowed the sensations to take over my body while I focused on the flames. A second later all I could hear were loud crunching noises as I was consumed with agony. My mouth opened and a scream left me. It was impossible to tell if my back arched because I could feel my bones stretching and changing position. My eyes blurred and I

FRENCH QUARTER FAE

lost sight of my sisters. The flames consumed me entirely and I lost focus of anything around me. Just when I thought I would die the pain stopped along with everything else.

My breath caught in my throat when the world came into focus, and I could see a bee flying toward a flower in the new garden the pixies had created. At the same time I saw that, I heard my sisters shouting my name. Kota's comment stood out above the others. "Shitballs, she's a damn dragon!"

That had actually worked. I'm a freaking dragon. There was a weight in the middle of my back making me wonder if I had wings. I turned my head to get a look. I was astonished by the light gray wings that extended behind me. My exam was cut short when I became dizzy. My head was far heavier and much higher than usual, disorienting me. A sparkle in the distance caught my eye consuming every ounce of my attention. My examination of my new reptilian body was forgotten as I took off running.

Within two strides I tripped over my feet and tumbled over getting tangled up in my wings. A loud trumpeting sound echoed out of my throat as I tried to track the sparkly object near the pixie mound. I needed whatever it was. It took several seconds to right myself. I noted how awkward movement was at the same time my mind obsessed on the shiny object.

Dahlia and Kota appeared to my right before I could take off again. Lia was waving her hands at me. "You need to shift back, Dani. Don't let the dragon take over."

Jelin hovered over her shoulder holding the shiny object in her hands. It was a beautiful piece of pink quartz. "Is this what you want?"

I lunged for the crystal. Lia and Kota screamed and dove to the side while Jelin dropped the object. I caught it in my palm before it hit the ground. Sitting on my haunches, I stared at the shiny object in my hand. I needed to find a place I could hide this and my other treasures.

Rage burned through me when Lia's hand reached for mine. I opened my mouth and trumpeted at the same time I pushed off the ground and tried to fly away. I panicked and the fire inside blasted from me and exited through my nostrils making me fall from the sky and sneeze. One of the rundown houses caught fire in the process.

The desire to protect my treasure was replaced by terror as I watched part of the property that I loved so much burn. Dropping the crystal, I watched in horror. A hand landed on my hide with a familiar energy signature. It was Phi. My other sisters were standing around her.

Kota wiped sweat from her forehead. "Shitballs, Dani. You scared the crap out of us."

Phi waved a hand at the burning house and chanted the spell to extinguish the flames. Once the fire was out, she turned and smiled at me. "No harm done. That house needed a complete overhaul anyway. Can you turn back?"

I focused on my regular body for several seconds, but nothing happened. My heart started racing again at the same time my eyes widened. I shook my head from side to side. Nothing was happening.

"Dani!" That was Noah's voice. His was followed by Kaitlyn calling out to me as they both ran from the main house toward us.

"What the hell happened?" Kaitlyn asked while Noah approached and put his hands on the sides of my face. I stood taller than him by about two feet.

"You're going to be alright, Sunshine. Focus on your human body and you'll shift back," Noah advised.

My eyes burned with tears. That wasn't working. I shook my head, frustrated by the situation. I wanted to tell him I needed another idea but I couldn't speak. Lia saved me when she shared her spot-on observations. "I don't think she can do that, Noah. She tried something before you arrived. What else can she do?"

Noah stepped back, giving him a better view of me. "Most shifters are born with an instinct about how to shift. I can feel how close to losing it you are, love. Try calming down. I don't know about dragons, but when our young have problems, we walk them through picturing every part of their body and if that fails our alphas can command them to turn back."

Kaitlyn opened a leather pouch and pulled out a vial filled with an orange potion. "This should force you to shift back. It works on feral shifters who refuse to cooperate with alphas. Is that alright with you, Dani?"

I nodded my head, knocking into Phi on accident. She fell into Dea and they went down. My wings twitched as I fought the desire to try and help them. The air from them making everyone but Noah take a couple of steps back. Kaitlyn didn't hesitate to toss the vial at me. I braced myself for the pain of the glass breaking on me only it never came. I heard the tinkle of the bottle breaking and squeezed my eyes shut.

A tingle began on my side and spread through my body. It was the magic of the liquid going to work. I kept thinking about my human body to ensure this worked. Unfortunately, nothing happened. I remained a dragon. My chest constricted and my chest started heaving. What if I was stuck as a dragon for the rest of my life? How would I survive like this? I couldn't do any of the things I loved. I couldn't even leave the plantation.

My head swiveled around searching for an answer. It was irrational. I knew there was nothing there that would help me. I should never have done something so stupid. Lia asked Kaitlyn if they should call Phoebe and ask about her friend that was mated to a dragon to see if he could help. The problem with that scenario is that they lived in England.

Noah got my attention again with a hand to one of my cheeks. I turned my big head slowly to avoid injuring anyone else. "Calm down, Sunshine. Getting upset about this is making it worse. You are not going to be stuck forever. We just need to figure out the key to dragons."

Lia rushed up to Noah's side waving her phone. "Aislin's mate, Argies said you need to focus on your human form while also dousing the fire in your core."

"It'll help if she has physical contact with her mate at the same time." A strange man's voice echoed from the speaker on Dahlia's cellphone. "He can keep her calm. The more agitated she is the harder it will be for her to transition."

I sucked in a deep breath, pulling oxygen into my lungs. It fed the flames in my chest making them grow, so I decided to hold my breath and imagine the lack of air smothering the flames. At the same time, I kept one of my eyes locked with Noah's. Picturing my human body was difficult until Noah lifted to his toes and kissed my scaly cheek. That reminded me of what he'd done to me the night before.

My body started tingling and my muscles moved around. The pain was less this time as my bones broke and shrank. My neck cracked along with my spine. I had to look like a pretzel with the way my body was contorting. It wasn't long before the wind blew through my shoulder length dirty blonde hair. I wiggled my fingers and looked down at my toes.

"I'm back!" My boobs bounced on my chest when I pumped a fist in the air. With a yelp, I pulled Noah in front of me. I had no clothes on! I knew that happened with Noah and Lucas but was so preoccupied I hadn't thought about it.

"I'll get you some clothes," Phi promised before she took off for the main house.

Noah looked over his shoulder at me before facing my sisters again. "Good work, Sunshine. Thank you for your help, Argies. I owe you for helping my mate."

Lia cleared her throat. "Yes, thank you, Argies. You're a lifesaver. If you need anything for the baby, let me know. We do custom signs for nurseries."

"Call anytime you need assistance. We will make some time to come out so I can work with the six of you sometime." Argies' offer surprised me. It would be a long trip for them with a newborn. "I'm curious how you have so many different species blended into your DNA."

Dahlia hung up the phone and returned it to her back pocket. I took the dress from Phi and tugged it over my head, hiding my nakedness. "It's a damn good thing we own so much property out here. That could have been a disaster. I won't be doing that again. I wanted to collect treasure and hoard it away somewhere. And I burned down one of our rental units! You don't think any of the mundies on Cami's tours saw, do you?"

Noah shook his head from side to side. "Don't worry, the view of this section of the property is obscured. But a more important matter is you saying you'll never shift again. You can't say that. You have a tool that might save your life one day. I don't care if you're in the middle of a mundie concert. You do whatever you need in order to survive."

Kota pointed at Noah. "I'm with him. We can deal with anything that happens later. Although, I'm not so sure I want to do more than shift my fingers."

I chuckled and leaned into Noah as he wrapped an arm around me. "Who all was able to shift?"

Phi lifted her chin with a self-satisfied smile on her face. "I managed talons and wings. Everyone else was able to do the talons."

Kaitlyn held up a hand. "Next time you want to try

shifting call me. I can be on hand to protect people and property."

"We'll be practicing this and offensive spells tomorrow, too," Dre informed Kaitlyn. "With Marie after us, we need to be able to defend ourselves and stop her."

"I'll be here," Kaitlyn promised.

Phi clapped her hands. "Now that that's settled, we should work on more of the signs for the anniversary party. It's happening soon."

I stifled my groan and gave Phi a thumbs up. I wanted to go in the house and relax while my body finished recovering but I wouldn't. I'd power through despite the fact that changing into a dragon was a brutal process and took a ton of energy.

CHAPTER 10

DAHLIA

Kip set her bag down on the coffee table in the Ladies' Parlor. "You ladies look better today. Especially you, Dani. Have you tried something in my absence?" Kaitlyn entered the room behind the healer.

"Would shifting into a dragon help? Because that's what we spent some time yesterday doing. Only Dani managed the full shift. The rest of us changed parts of our bodies," Kota shared as she sipped a passionfruit lemonade that she had made for Cami's tours today. The last one ended a half an hour earlier.

Dea started laughing at the bewildered look on Kip's face. Relief washed over me as everyone else started laughing along with Dea. Since our powers were unlocked, Dea discovered that she was an empath as well as a psychic of sorts. She could see ghosts that no one else could see. Her ability wasn't limited to the visual. She also had the ability to send spirits to the other side. A few weeks ago, Pap Legba nearly claimed Dea's body. This was the first time since then that she was truly herself.

Cami entered the room in her modern clothes with a smile on her face and Lucas and Noah in tow. "What'd I miss?"

I smiled at the former slave as Lucas pressed a kiss to the top of my head and took a position behind my chair. Camilla was a witch that lived and died hundreds of years ago. Phoebe's magic brought her back from the dead as a ghoul and we adopted her. We also reunited her body with her soul making her whole once again. "Kota was telling Kip about Dani's shifting yesterday."

Cami's brow furrowed. "I'm glad all we could smell here was the smoke. I surely would not have had an answer for the mundies if they asked why there was a fire breathing dragon on the plantation."

Kaitlyn tapped her lips. "Perhaps you should stop the tours while the sisters are learning their powers."

Cami gasped and her lower lip started trembling. My heart went out to her. I shook my head as I met the head witch's stare. "That's not happening. The tours are Cami's project. Not only does she conduct them, she's done all the work creating them. We will be more careful and never shift during business hours."

Dani picked up one of the candle holders from the fireplace mantle and held it. Noah hovered close to her, ready to catch her if she got sucked into a memory. Dani had been touching things more and more since we got out of Marie's dungeon. I liked seeing her use the tactics that we'd discussed while being held captive. And it was a huge relief to see her training herself to hold her psychometric power back so she could skim over memories and not get sucked into them. I knew she felt like a freak having to wear gloves everywhere.

Setting the holder back down, Dani nodded her head in agreement with me. "We aren't stopping our practices and we aren't canceling the tours. Tourists love Cami. Besides, we know more now. And the back of our property is pretty well hidden. We can have the pixies establish taller vegetation if the need arises. I'd rather go back to Kip's question. Is it possible the shifting has helped us?"

Kip inclined her head and rolled with the flow of conversation easily. "I'd say it's definitely the reason. Shifters age slower and have better healing capabilities. I'd like to examine you both to get a better idea."

Dani sat on the edge of the coffee table and clasped her hands together. She might be pushing herself in our house, but she wasn't ready to go there with people yet. Kip approached my sister, stood next to her, then placed one of her hands by her chest and the other by her back. The healer closed her light green eyes and chanted under her breath.

The room remained quiet while she did her work. When she opened her eyes several seconds later, she was smiling. "Your dragon DNA is much more prominent now which is a good thing. I don't sense any remnants of Marie's curse in your system. Let's check you out, Dahlia."

I nodded and shifted forward in my chair. Kip repeated the process while I held my breath and prayed for good news. While my energy level had improved, I still got tired easily. And the wrinkles around my eyes were deeper than before. My hair was back to the regular platinum blonde thanks to Dani's quick dye job the night before. Heat radiated from the healer and spread through my veins. I imagined little nanobots seeking out damaged cells and repairing them when found.

I had a grimace on my face when Kip opened her eyes. Her smile wasn't quite as bright when she looked at me. I sighed and rubbed my temples to stave off the headache the tension was bringing on. "I'm the same, right? Is this curse eventually going to kill me?"

Lucas's hand squeezed my shoulder. "We will find a solution for all of you. Don't worry, Flower."

Kip took a bottle with the same bright blue potion she'd given us a few times already. "There's nothing to worry about, Lia. I still feel particles from the curse in your system, however it's dormant. The potion should keep it that way until you can shift and burn the rest of it away."

I accepted the vial and downed the contents thinking about how we needed to stop Voodoo Queen, once and for all. "I've been thinking about how we can beat Marie. I think our best bet is to create the Aegis Council where the leaders of each faction come together to ensure the safety for the entire magical population in New Orleans. Things have been unregulated which gave Marie the power she has today. We've been chipping away at it, but with the Dark Fae joining forces with her, we've taken several steps in the wrong direction. The way I see it, we have more than half a dozen leaders on board already. That is if you count the six of us as separate. I'm not really sure where we stand. Regardless, with the shifters, witches, and necromancers on board it should be possible."

Lucas came around the chair so I could see his profile. Warmth filled me when I saw that he was beaming with pride. "You mean like a regulatory committee?"

"That's one way to look at it. Basically, the leaders would act as a check and balance to make sure no one gains control over a smaller faction like Marie did. It levels the playing field and provides another layer to encourage powerful supernaturals to behave. Who would want to get on the bad side of the Aegis Council?"

Lucas gestured to Kaitlyn. "This is brilliant. I've wondered what it would take to do something like this for years. It's bothered me for some time that Laveau has as much power as she does. I've never said anything because, honestly, it felt hopeless. My mate humbles me with her courage to tackle this head on."

One of Kaitlyn's eyebrows rose on her forehead. "We have the gargoyles and sirens on our side, as well. I'm sure you can convince Brezok to talk to the demons about joining." The head witch shook her head from side to side. "You six are something else. You've made connections and formed alliances with more factions in six months than I have in my entire life. I like the idea of people like Marie having to answer to a council for overstepping and trying to assume power that doesn't belong to her. Lucas is right about feeling hopeless. I've cowed to Marie since taking this position. I've even cast wards around her lair to keep her hidden from the loa and other enemies when I didn't want to. It's about damn time we stood up to her."

"Not all of the factions have an official leader. I'll call Albar and Nedasea and let them know they need a representative. Talewen can call the pixies together so they can select a leader to represent them. Drake can bring the Fae together," Lucas added. I wondered how much clout our DJ had among his fellow Fae.

"I'll call Talindra and have her speak with the elves to elect a leader," Noah offered.

Lucas looked at Kaitlyn. "Who's going to call Viktor?"

Kaitlyn was shaking her head when Phi gasped and her eyes rolled back in her head. "The djinn presents an obstacle for the head witch to overcome. The clock is ticking on this particular mating dance. By the new moon the Voodoo Queen will reclaim her power and eliminate her enemies." My sister's words came out in a deep, monotone voice. Nothing like she typically sounds.

I gaped at the baby of the family. "What the hell just happened? Did she just predict the future?"

Kaitlyn sat forward and examined Phi's face. "Delphine, it seems, is a seer. Where you get a clear vision of what is to come, she is given a message. Most often they're cryptic and need to be deciphered. This one is no different."

Kota snorted. "It seemed pretty clear to me. You have to do a mating dance with a genie in order to get this council established."

Dre nudged Kota's shoulder while the rest of us laughed. I blamed Dea because, as usual, she started it. Phi shook like a fish out of water for a split second before her eyes snapped open. "What happened?"

Dre's face furrowed as she clasped Phi's hand. "You just delivered a prophecy, sestra. It seems that you're a seer."

"What?" Delphine exclaimed as she jumped to her feet. "What does that mean?"

Kaitlyn's expression was a mix between puzzled and annoyed when she looked at Phi. "What do you remember from a few seconds ago?"

Delphine clutched the iPad that was sitting in her lap. "The last thing I recall was Lucas asking who was going to call the head vampire."

Kaitlyn sighed. "Being a seer means that you will go into trances and receive information about the future from time to time."

Phi's eyes went wide and she sat forward. "How do I control it? I can't get spacey and recite some nonsense when I'm lecturing." Delphine was a biochemistry professor at Tulane. "Wait, what did I say anyway?"

Dakota chuckled. "You mentioned something about Kaitlyn needing to do a mating dance with a djinn."

Phi collapsed back into the chair with a sigh. "I can't go

around talking about paranormals. They'd lock me in an insane asylum."

Kaitlyn inclined her head. "I appreciate your position. However, I'm not aware of a seer being able to control when they get visions. I'll do some research and reach out to the known seers in the states."

Lucas held up a hand. "In the meantime, you will need to connect with the Djinn. Noah and I will approach Viktor."

"What is a djinn anyway?"

Kaitlyn pursed her lips and glowered. "They're dangerous and tricky. The djinn aren't genies that grant wishes. They're powerful beings capable of a wide variety of magic but they will only perform them in exchange for favors owed to them. They don't collect right away and you have to negotiate terms or they can ask you for literally anything. Djinn become more powerful in their society based on the number of favors they've accumulated."

Lucas nodded his head. "One of the first things we teach our young is not to deal with the djinn. They prey on the uninformed and manipulate to get what they want from a person. The more desperate you are for their help, the more they will be able to squeeze out of you."

Kaitlyn ran a hand through her hair. "I should have known the djinn would come to bite me in the ass. I've been waiting my entire life for one of them to show up on my doorstep."

"Why's that?" Dre asked.

Kaitlyn's expression turned sheepish. "I inherited a debt from a five- or six-times great-grandmother. She wanted to catch the eye of a rich mage in town. The problem was that he didn't see her because she came from a poor family. Which was why she enlisted the help of a djinn. I won't have to give up my wealth or children when the marker comes due. Other than that, I'm not sure what will be asked of me."

Kip lifted her bag from the table. "I, too, owe the djinn a favor. Only for me, it wasn't because of the stupidity of an ancestor. I made the deal. It was years ago. I needed to have my healing abilities enhanced to save my sister who was mortally wounded. It was a one-time thing and I still owe Kaveh a favor for it."

Lucas, Noah, and Cami all gasped at the same time. Lucas extended a hand in Kip's direction. "How is that possible? Marie forbade the djinn from operating within the city before I was born."

Cami nodded her head. "That dates back to my time. I recall mother talking about the magic Marie stole to block them."

Kip's head jerked in surprise. "There was an actual spell warding the city from their presence? I thought they weren't around because the knowledge of how to summon them was destroyed by Marie. Or so she thought. My family kept our grimoire hidden and the information blocked so it couldn't be found. How was I able to summon Kaveh to my house?"

Kaitlyn lifted a shoulder as she looked off in the distance. "My guess is that Marie hasn't been able to renew it as needed. She was at her peak in power hundreds of years ago. However, witches and other paranormals have discovered ways to protect themselves from her traps. Few ever fall into any of them anymore. In fact, it's been a decade since I've encountered any new ones. That was when she forced the necromancers under her thumb."

"Necros aren't as powerful as witches. She's been losing power for hundreds of years. It's why she needed those wards. Her loa are pissed at her for failing to live up to her end of the bargain," Kip added.

My brain rifled through the information I'd learned about the Voodoo Queen. The original Marie Laveau made a deal with the voodoo loa for power in exchange for various favors. Much like the arrangement with a djinn. If I wasn't mistaken, Samedi required innocent souls as a sacrifice as well as time on Earth in a corporeal body so he can indulge in his habits.

"What was Kaveh like?" Kaitlyn asked.

Kip lifted her hands above her shoulders and tilted her head from side to side. "Kaveh was the second in command to the djinn leader at the time. He's gorgeous. Tall, muscular with dark brown skin that has this magical glow about it. He's also arrogant and full of himself. However, he was fair when I dealt with him. Aside from the same stuff about money and off-spring, he agreed the favor would not put me in a dangerous position and that he would never ask me to trade places with him."

Kaitlyn nodded her head. "He doesn't sound so bad. Stories about the powerful djinn leader setting up my great-whatever grandmother for heartbreak abounded in my family."

"I don't understand? I thought he helped her get the rich mage's attention," Dea said.

Kaitlyn chuckled but the sound was strained. "Yes, he did do that. However, he didn't guarantee the guy would fall in love with her. The spell lasted long enough for the guy to sleep with my great-grandmother. When he came to his senses, she was pregnant and he shunned her. Back then premarital sex was a sin and she was cast out of town. She gave birth to her daughter in a hut in the swamps while vowing to get revenge on those who had wronged her."

That was underhanded. I wondered if the djinn made the guy turn away from her grandma. I thought guys did the right thing back in the day. "Did the djinn make the mage turn away from her? Can you negotiate that they can't interfere with whatever they're helping you with?"

"You can try to negotiate that and should. From what I've

learned there are far too many issues to consider when negotiating with a djinn which is why it's best to steer clear of them," Lucas replied.

Kaitlyn nodded her head. "Absolutely. And, no one knows if the djinn interfered but men typically lived up to their responsibilities during that time. There were other things that convinced her the djinn played her, like being cast out of town. Often a family could hide such conditions until the child was born. Of course, she would have had to leave the baby at a church to maintain her standing in the community."

Lucas rubbed his hands together. "That's enough discussion about the djinn. We need to invite them to be a part of the council. They have a beef with Laveau and should be eager for the chance to cull her power. She's the only person I know of that has crossed them in such an egregious manner. We all know who we have to contact and the timeframe in which to do it. We'll get together again in a few days for a progress report."

Everyone agreed, then Kaitlyn and Kip took their leave while I was lost in my head. The thought of bringing the djinn into this council made me uncomfortable. I didn't like the idea of owing someone a favor without clear parameters. However, that didn't mean they should be excluded. They deserved a chance to have some of their freedoms back. I couldn't imagine being banned from New Orleans for so long. It would also be nice to show Marie she'd lost even more power by bringing them in.

The magical population of our city needed to be warned about making deals with djinn and I would find a way to do that. Perhaps, I would even talk to Lucas about adding a clause in the council bylaws that prohibited anyone from soliciting favors from others.

The enormity of the task ahead of us hit me fully and I was grateful that my sisters and I had made as many friends in this world as we had. It paid to be talented and throw kickass parties.

CHAPTER 11

DANIELLE

"Why exactly are we here with you?" Delphine asked as Lia parked the car in Ricky's lot.

Free parking downtown was becoming a major perk of being the fated ones to the pack alpha and his beta. Dahlia and I seemed to have meetings with clients several times a week in the Quarter since we opened Willowberry, which meant that parking at Ricky's had saved us at least a grand in the past few months.

Kaitlyn smiled at Phi as we all climbed out of the SUV. "Because we want to watch you closely to see if you go into anymore trances. That potion I gave you to block your third eye might not have worked. I still think it's unwise to inhibit such a power. You've been given it for a reason and trying to circumvent that might backfire."

Lia handed Ricky her keys and thanked him for keeping her car next to his tiny shack. "I get your fear, Phi, but I think Kaitlyn might be right. It's dangerous to stifle our energy.

FRENCH QUARTER FAE

You can take a short leave of absence and we can work on your control."

I considered how I'd been doing my own version of stopping my ability. I'd been wearing gloves everywhere, even in my house, for months. It had only been the past few days, after being rescued from Marie's dungeon, that I'd begun trying to train myself how not to get sucked into memories. I'd gotten to the point that I hovered above memories contained in objects, taking in some of the details and emotions, without being pulled into the middle of it as if I was the person experiencing the event. And here I was, walking to a bar in the Quarter to meet the leader of the djinn without gloves.

I clapped Phi on the shoulder keeping out of the memory of Tucker kissing her goodbye earlier that morning. "I know how scary it is, sestra. No one knows if it's possible for you to stop the visions, but you might be able to get to the point where you can receive enough of a warning to excuse yourself. I would be relegated to gloves still if I didn't open myself to possibilities like Lia suggested. Her suggestions gave me hope and worked wonders."

Phi grimaced and inclined her head. "How is that going anyway? You seem to be doing better but I can't tell for sure."

I beamed at her and explained how I'd only been focusing on keeping myself above the memories. "I'm going with my gut on this one and using one strategy at a time. The biggest risk for me is when I become immersed, because the real world disappears and I'm left vulnerable. This way I'm able to stay cognizant of both."

Kaitlyn's brow furrowed. "I haven't been the best leader for you six. I should have found individuals that can help you cope with your abilities. I'm accustomed to parents handling that for their children. I'll search for a seer to help you, Phi. Just as soon as we handle the djinn. We can't afford for you to reveal the existence of the magical world, but we don't want to limit your life, either."

Phi dipped her head as she tilted her head to look at Kaitlyn. "I appreciate that. I've considered doing something different but I enjoy teaching. I'd appreciate it if you can ask if there are any books that I can study to teach me more, as well." Phi was a scholar and learned best when she had information to read that backed up lessons. I was a visual learner and did best when I watched how to do something.

"I look forward to working with someone experienced with smell-o-vision but right now, I want to be sure we're prepared for the djinn," Lia interjected as we ducked into a courtyard off Royal Street that was hidden behind a hedge.

The concrete sidewalk gave way to a tiled patio showcasing a sizeable fountain. The surrounding building was two stories high, and the stucco was painted a terracotta color. There were plants and trees everywhere. It was a stunning escape from the crowded city a few feet away.

Unlike the first time Lia and I visited the Final Swallow, I wasn't nervous as Kaitlyn opened the wood door. I turned my gaze to Phi and watched her take in the scene. I imagined she was surprised that the bar was vastly different from the beautiful courtyard outside, while also being similar to just about every other bar we'd ever been inside. That is if you overlooked Brezok, the fame demon that owned the place and was standing behind the long, wooden bar. Bottles of alcohol stood like soldiers on the shelves behind him.

Phi lifted a hand and waved at the demon. Brezok had worked several parties at the plantation, so she was familiar with his spade-tipped red tail, black eyes and horns. "What can I get the beautiful Smith sisters today?" Brezok's voice was deep.

"I'll take a Sprite. We're meeting with Kaveh. Not here to unwind this trip," Kaitlyn told the fame demon.

Phi ordered lemonades for us as I scanned the dimly lit room, skimming the high-top tables. There was no stage or dance floor full of closely packed bodies. The place was filled with wooden tables with seating for four people, but I had no idea who we were looking for.

Brezok leaned over the bar top toward us. "Next time you want to meet with a banned demon, don't use my joint. I can't afford to piss Marie off. She'll have my balls."

I wanted to tell him that he needed to buck up, that we were doing something about her while most were content to sit back and let the status quo continue. Kaitlyn patted Brezok's red hand. "We'll keep that in mind. Although, it's not likely going to be an issue long. Things are changing, which brings me to a second reason for being here. I'm not sure if Lucas has reached out to you, but Dahlia had a brilliant idea to give every group a voice in the city. We're forming a council and we need demons to elect a representative. Can I count on you to bring them together so you all can select that person? We're having the first meeting of the Aegis Council next week."

Brezok's face contorted into a terrifying grimace. Given the way his mouth parted, I assumed that was his surprised face. Brezok blinked and his face cleared. "I don't know whether you're stupid or incredibly brave. The six of you have shaken up the way life works for the paranormal community here in New Orleans."

Lia lifted one corner of her mouth and one eyebrow at the demon. "Hopefully, the changes are for the better for most."

Brezok laughed. "That has yet to be determined. I'd be happy to call my brethren together. I'm anxious to see where this goes. It would be nice to finally have a voice. There's your djinn. Can you get your meeting over with, so my customers aren't so anxious?"

I rolled my eyes as I took in the crowd. None of them were looking at the man sitting alone at a table across the bar. Even sitting down, I could tell that Kaveh was a tall guy. His long, graceful fingers wrapped around a pint of dark beer. I was mesmerized by his good looks as we crossed the space. He had black hair, brown eyes, and a perfect bronze complexion with full lips. It was a face you'd see on the cover of magazines. He stood up as we approached. His impossibly long legs were covered with jeans and a plain blue t-shirt was over his slender but muscular torso. Looking down, I was not surprised to see thick soled boots on the guy.

His intense brown eyes focused on Kaitlyn. He extended his hand to her. "You must be Kaitlyn. I was glad to get your call. My clan has been curious about the changes we've felt in this city recently."

Kaitlyn clasped his hand. "And you're Kaveh. These are my friends, Danielle, Delphine, and Dahlia. Are you the leader of the djinn? I need to speak with someone that can make decisions for your clan."

Kaveh didn't let go of Kaitlyn. Instead, his fingers wrapped around her hand and he held on to her. "I took over four years ago."

Kaitlyn yanked her hand out of his and wiped it on her pants before she moved around the table. "Shall we sit? We have much to discuss."

Kaveh acted as if we didn't exist. He took the chair he'd been sitting in before while Kaitlyn took the one next to him. Lia took a chair from the table next to us and the rest of us took a seat. It was a tight fit with the five of us around the small wood square. Kaveh wrapped his fingers around his beer again and met Kaitlyn's gaze. "If this is about the Aegis Council that I heard you mention to Brezok I can say we aren't interested. The djinn learned long ago it's better to keep to ourselves. I will watch from the sidelines. I, too, am curious to see where this goes. I won't get my people caught up in this mess."

Kaitlyn frowned and narrowed her eyes on Brezok. "Things are changing here. Don't you want to be in on the changes? I imagine your people miss living in the city."

Kaveh's eyes heated as he looked at Kaitlyn. "I admit that I find myself drawn here. There are so many, uh, beautiful things to see and appreciate. However, I cannot risk my kind being persecuted again for who they are."

Dahlia slapped her hands on the table then paused as a guy dropped our drinks off. I didn't see Nedasea working. She must have had the day off. Lia slid her glass toward her spot and held Kaveh's gaze. "My sisters and I are new to the magical world, so correct me if I'm wrong, but I believe djinn thrive on collecting favors and that Marie stopped you from providing services in exchange for favors. That wasn't something she ever should have done. The djinn aren't the only ones she's taken control over. The necromancers used to have to dance to the tune she directed. Now, they're free to do as they please."

Kaveh's expression was a lot less friendly when he focused on Lia. "From what I've heard there is no real freedom. Marie's power reaches further than you know. She's let you see an illusion that she can't command the necromancers anymore. I'm surprised a powerful witch like yourself is listening to the suggestions of individuals that are little more than mundies."

Lia scoffed and gestured to the room around us. "Your bias keeps you from seeing the strength in us. We might be supernatural mutts but we're more powerful than you can imagine. We've survived a hex Marie Laveau cast on us, an attack by a skin walker, being cut up in a voodoo ritual and Samedi's possession. The paranormals here are taking back their power. Are you too chicken to grab a place for your kind?"

I struggled to keep from smacking my sister. What was she thinking, pissing off the powerful djinn? No one wanted them having freedom to manipulate paranormals that wouldn't know how to negotiate with them. I tensed, expecting him to smite us, or something. Instead, the djinn leader gaped at my sister. "You survived one of Marie's curses?"

Dahlia pointed to the wrinkles that had deepened beside her eyes. "She kidnapped Dani and I almost four days ago and I am fighting off the last of the hex now." Lia gestured to me. "There's no remnants of the curse in her anymore."

I could see her words softening Kaveh, so I jumped in. "We also kept her magic from affecting us for two days. Plus, we found a way to get a signal out past her wards."

I could feel the power when Kaveh's brown eyes focused on me. This guy had some serious magic under his sleeve. "I can see the evidence of your claims. You three aren't what you seem at all."

Phi lifted a hand. "Umm, there's six of us. We're the Six Twisted Sisters and we run the Willowberry Plantation."

Kaveh's forehead wrinkled as he turned his gaze on Phi then chuckled. "I like your gumption. I'll join the meeting. I can see with these twisted sisters' involvement that we stand a chance. And Lia, I would like to offer you a favor for including my kind in the process."

Dahlia's cheeks heated and she clasped her hands around her glass of untouched lemonade. "I didn't actually tell them who to involve. I admit when I heard your kind existed, I immediately wanted you involved because of what you've been through. I'm also wary. Your services come with strings."

"I had a premonition, or vision that you would do some

kind of a dance with Kait, um never mind," Phi said as she clamped her mouth shut.

Kaitlyn's face was as red as a beet. To her credit, she moved right past Phi's comment. "Lia, none of us would be having this conversation without your suggestion. This offer is unprecedented and one of the most powerful things you could receive. Djinn never do this."

Dahlia nodded and smiled at Kaveh. "Thank you?" Her voice rose at the end as if she were asking a question.

Kaveh shook his head then began rubbing his hands together so fast it sent out ripples of energy. Light sparked inside his palms as he continued the action while focusing on Phi of all people. I would have expected him to look at Kaitlyn. It had been obvious he was attracted to her. The energy buffered against me as if it was a sail being blown by the wind. It wasn't constant but intermittent.

Sweat broke out across Kaveh's forehead as his eyebrows pulled together in the middle. He grunted and shook as if he was dead lifting a car. His energy cut off before rebounding back to him. This time it was a steady flow with minor ebbs every couple of seconds. The cords on the side of his neck stood out as he poured more energy into what he was doing.

Lia gave me her 'what the hell is going on' look. I lifted a shoulder in response. I was clueless as to what the djinn leader was doing. He could be trying to maintain his presence in the bar for all I knew. No one told us exactly what the Laveau hex did to the djinn aside from preventing them from using their magic in New Orleans. The mere idea that she was capable of something like that seemed daunting. We were trying to put her in her place and take her down a ladder of pegs.

My panic ended before it ever got started when Kaveh's hands began to glow a deep blue. Those lights spread out and began swirling around his arms like a whirlwind. I had to lift my hand to shield my eyes from the brightness. And his energy was a constant presence moving against me. The display got everyone's attention. My nerves jumped when conversation stopped as all eyes focused on our table. The silence didn't last long. The bar patrons began murmuring questioning about how the djinn was able to perform magic in the city.

Kaveh was panting and sucking oxygen into his lungs when he stopped using his magic. His posture sagged against the table and sweat trickled down his temples. He looked like he'd run around the world just then. The djinn leader lifted a clenched hand a couple of feet above the table. He extended his arm to Phi and opened his fingers. A green peridot stone sat on his palm. With a birthday in August, the charm matched her birth stone. Making that had taken a lot out of him.

Kaveh thrust his open palm at Phi. "Take it. The stone is enchanted to alert you when a premonition is coming. And Marie's magic is difficult to work through but not impossible. It's why it took me so long to create this charm."

What the hell? I gaped at the guy. "Can you read minds or something?" How had he picked up on precisely what I was wondering?

Kaveh chuckled and shook his head. "In a manner of speaking. My kind is able to pick up on what a person wants most. It's instinct for us." I bet they used it to up the cost of their favors. They would know how desperate a person was to get their hands on something. "Consider this an indicator of good faith on my part. I'm not agreeing to this because I am looking for a way for my people to have open access to the paranormals in this city. I want to be part of equalizing the power for everyone living here. There's been an imbalance for too long."

His comment made me wonder about a thousand

different things. How exactly did paranormal beings gather their powers? Was Marie so powerful because of the hold she had over so many supernatural factions? It seemed like a good theory to me, given a djinn had more magic the more favors they owned. That was like a way of harnessing a piece of that person. And if Kaitlyn still had her great-grandmother's debt after centuries, it seemed they rarely called in these markers. It totally fit. Marie was somehow getting power by keeping so many under her thumb.

Kaveh looked around the bar. "I must take my leave now. Text the location of meeting Katy. My number is in your phone. And thank you for including us. I'm at your service should you need it, Dahlia."

Kaitlyn looked stunned as the djinn leader kissed the back of her hand, then left the bar. Dahlia teased the head witch about the mating dance that had begun between the two. Delphine was running a finger over the peridot charm Kaveh had given her. That solved one major problem for her. Still, my gut was in knots over this.

I hated the feeling of uneasiness that talking with the djinn left me with. They were extremely powerful, and yet, Marie Laveau and her descendants had managed to keep them from practicing in her city for centuries. That was no easy feat for anyone. I was part of the magical world now and had no desire to have the Voodoo Queen control what I was able to do. And I wasn't moving.

"Do you think we can strip enough power from Marie by forming this council? We need to make sure she can't continue posing a threat to the magical population but I'm not sure how having this group will stop her," I admitted. I would love to remove the target from my back, as well. However, that wasn't as important as making sure no one else fell victim to Marie and fed into her power.

Kaitlyn lifted one shoulder. "The more I've thought about

it, the more I can see that Lia was right. This will be our best bet. Aside from reaching out to the factions about electing a leader, I've been hunting down every scrap of information I can on Marie Laveau. From every obscure document that ever mentioned her to books and grimoires. Every witch I know is looking through their family book of shadows for any information about Marie. I haven't discovered much yet, but collectively we can keep her from draining energy that the paranormals imbue in our surroundings simply by living here."

Phi gestured to me and Lia with her glass. "I need to add the details about what happened to you two to our grimoire. I didn't even think of documenting something like that, but it could help future generations to know."

Kaitlyn clapped Phi on her shoulder. "That's precisely the type of thing you should include. It's not only potion ingredients and spells that can be helpful."

I considered what we'd been through over the past few months. That book we bought should be full by now. "Thank you for keeping our book of shadows up to date, sestra. We've had enough encounters to make your fingers cramp from all the writing."

Phi clenched and unclenched her fingers. "Tell me about it. The skin walker situation filled a dozen pages alone. I'm not looking forward to going back and adding the zombie attacks, the siren insurgence and the pixies. Is there a spell that can write it for us?"

"There is a spell. But it tends to leave information out, so you will want to double check the details and fill in the blanks," Kaitlyn replied. Phi opened her notes app on her phone as the head witch continued. "You will want to use *scribere ad locuti verbum* on your pen before you recount the details, and it will write them down."

Phi typed the information into her phone. "That'll come

in handy and make getting caught up easier. I want to be prepared to add new information as we go through this process."

I was still skeptical that forming this council would make our lives easier or better. Marie Laveau was a larger-than-life villain backed by powerful loa. The council wouldn't turn Marie's attempts to make things away. They wanted what she could give them. And she'd been meeting her end of the bargain for centuries. What chance did this baby council stand against that?

These species coming together is an historic event and it's going to be the pin that pops the balloon. I swear my inner voice sounded like our mother just now. I wanted to believe that she was talking to me and helping me keep a positive attitude, like she used to when she was alive. Even if it was all in my head, I was going to cling to that message until I saw different.

CHAPTER 12

DAHLIA

Brezok came around the bar and clapped me on the shoulder. "I'm happy to say I managed to convince over ninety percent of the demons to attend a meeting here after closing tonight. Convincing Kaveh to join won you major points with them."

I lifted one eyebrow at the red-skinned devil. "That's good news. Are you putting yourself up for nomination?" I'd like to know what kind of demon we will have join us on the council.

Brezok shook his head from side to side. "Nah. I'm busy enough here and with your events. Besides I don't need to ask to know it won't pay anything. Nothing like that ever does. It'll probably be Molvith. Tanarak will make a play for it no doubt, but no one wants a rage demon acting as the leader for such a volatile species."

The casual way he spoke about having a rage demon was terrifying. They didn't sound like the kind of beings we wanted on Earth at all. "Well, keep me posted. We will see you for the anniversary party, right?"

Brezok held up a paper calendar. "I'll be there with bells on."

We said goodbye to the fame demon and left the Final Swallow. I shivered when the moon shone down on us as we walked outside. I thought it would be daytime when we left. We'd gone in later in the afternoon and hadn't been in there long. How long had it taken Kaveh to make that stone for Phi, anyway? It hadn't seemed like more than five or ten minutes.

Phi shoved her peridot in her front pocket. "I'm glad the djinn are on our side. I wouldn't want to make an enemy of them. Kaveh was one scary dude. Good looking, but frightening. And it seems my premonition was right. The sexual tension between the two of you could be cut with a knife."

Kaitlyn choked and stumbled making the rest of us laugh. The head witch wagged a finger at us. "You need to stop that shit. I'm perfectly happy without the complications of a man. And I certainly don't need one as controversial as a djinn."

There was something in Kaitlyn's voice that hinted at more. There were countless reasons for a woman not to want a man's attention. The question was why Kaitlyn was opposed to this and if it was something I should help her overcome. "What's wrong with a djinn? Are they violent? Do they have nasty kinks?"

Kaitlyn rolled her eyes and turned right down Royal Street. "Djinn are notorious playboys. Kaveh is said to be one of the worst. No thank you. I have enough bullshit in my life without adding more. I'm perfectly happy being alone."

"That doesn't mean he will continue to be that way. I've known many men and women who have had meaningless sex night after night with different people because they hadn't found the right one for them," Dani countered.

I nodded in agreement as we passed a tour group of mundies. "You need to keep an open mind where Kaveh is concerned. You never know what might come of it. Phi's visions are closer to prophecies which tells me fate is at work here. You wouldn't want to piss off the gods, would you?"

Kaitlyn snorted as she cut down the alley next to the church where Lucas and I had seen the loa Samedi. "Can we set this aside for now. I can't even think about Kaveh when we are worried about convincing the other factions to join the council. This will only work if we present a unified front."

There was no way I would push her about this when I had been in her shoes not long ago. I hadn't wanted to talk about what was brewing between Lucas and I, let alone acknowledge it. I held my hands up in the air, letting her know I was dropping that subject. "So, have you talked to Tempe, yet? I was curious who the necros voted as their rep."

"I assumed you would do that since she saved your life and you guys seem to be tight," Kaitlyn admitted.

I'd suspected that was the case. I'd been a bit preoccupied by trying to shift into a dragon and get rid of the rest of Marie's hex. It wasn't about getting rid of the wrinkles anymore, either. They were a sign of what I had survived. It was the fatigue that got me. It made me worry the curse would kick into high gear at any moment and take me out. I'd just started the second act of my life and I wasn't ready to call it quits yet.

A high-pitched scream rent the air making all four of us race through the alley for Jackson Square. Usually, I was one of the first in the group. Thanks to the hex, I was last to arrive. My heart nearly jumped out of my chest when I saw the reason for the scream.

There were a half a dozen pointy-eared men snarling at mundies. A seventh had his arms wrapped around a woman's chest, pinning her arms at her sides. All of them were tall and skinny like the Dark Fae working with Marie.

"Are they elves?" Phi whispered to our group.

I cursed when her question got their attention. Kaitlyn and Dani immediately started chanting a spell that would freeze the mundies surrounding the square while I ran forward to meet one of the Dark Elves near the wrought iron fence surrounding the small garden area.

A sharp wind knocked me off balance, sending me flying into the posts. The elf was on me a second later. I was already in the process of conjuring my witch fire and didn't let my fear stop me. Amber flames danced over my hands. I chucked a ball at an elf coming up behind the one that was waving a dagger at me. I threw the flames from my other hand and aimed for the odd weapon that glowed with a dark light and had strange symbols carved into the sides. They looked like runes or old Norse letters.

The blade sliced open the skin above my right breast, leaving a trail of agony as it went. A growl left me as I ducked and punched out at the guy's groin. I managed to connect with his balls at the same time I heard Lucas calling my name. My heart raced as I considered him being in danger at the same time, I loved him even more for always being there for me. I wondered how he was there when I needed him most. A thought popped into my head. He must sense when I'm in trouble through our bond.

I felt it growing by leaps and bounds every day. He brought me an energy drink the other day, while I was in the laser silo doing cups for the anniversary party, a few seconds after I had the thought that I needed one. It was crazy, exhilarating, and came in handy. He said it would get even stronger after we completed the mating ritual. Perhaps I should go ahead with that sooner rather than later. It might have directed him to me while Marie was holding me hostage. That was a consideration for another time.

I shifted my hands into talons and swiped the sharp claws at the asshole. I danced around him while thinking about shifting fully into a dragon. I could chow down and the mundies that saw anything would never remember it.

I saw a ripple in the air before several figures appeared in my periphery. That wasn't good. How the hell many could be hiding around us right now? Lucas's howl filled the air letting me know he was now in his wolf form. The elf that was fighting me went down under his massive gray wolf. Blood flew as Lucas ripped the elf's throat out and moved on. I took the chance to look around and noticed everyone was fighting a Dark Elf or Dark Fae.

"How did you know we were here?" Dani shouted at Noah as she tossed her yellow flames at the elf she was fighting.

"We've been hunting Dark Fae all night. They keep popping up in the Quarter," Noah replied.

The number of Fae fighting us dwindled rapidly and I was able to move closer to Dani. I didn't actually reach her because I was hit from behind by something small. It smacked into the back of my head and I stumbled forward, landing on my hands and knees. The impact sent pain shooting up my thighs and arms. That was going to hurt like a bitch later.

Temperence ran out of the exit from Pirates Alley. The necromancer cursed as she rushed to my side and helped me up. "What the hell was that?"

I turned and scanned the area. "I'm not sure. It felt like a boulder."

Tempe gasped and pointed to a tree in the closed garden area. "I bet it was that rock creature. I've never seen anything like it."

I grabbed her and shoved her to the side so the rock coming at her couldn't hurt her. The projectile was a light tan color unlike the dark gray of the thing that had hit me. I leaped into the air as high as my stubby legs would carry me and swung my arm with all my might. I managed to bat the thing away with my talons. One broke on the hard surface. To my surprise, it landed with a thud on the sidewalk and didn't move. It looked like nothing more than a regular rock.

Temperence righted herself and turned to face the Fae that probably sent the rock in her direction. "These Fae have been going nuts all over the French Quarter tonight. I had to cancel my tours. Where the hell did they come from?"

The guy facing her snarled, revealing stained teeth. Why did bad guys have such poor dental hygiene? "We came from Eidothea to claim your planet as ours."

My energy was fading fast. I prayed it lasted long enough to get us out of trouble. I lurched away as Tempe yelled something at a Fae. The two grappled with one another, throwing punches and kicks. I turned to locate the rock creature in the tree but it was gone. A hand grabbed a fistful of hair and yanked me to the ground while I was preoccupied.

I lost a chunk of my signature platinum blonde locks but managed to yank free of the elf that had me. I still had my talons and swiped them up, slicing the guy's thigh and coming perilously close to his groin.

His eyes flew wide, and he stopped moving. "Bitch, you almost gelded me."

I lifted a shoulder and threw a ball of amber flames at the guy before he could recover. He tried to bat them away as he fought me. The fist that connected with the side of my head rung my bell good. My legs were shaky, my arms hurt, and now I was seeing stars. Thankfully, my flames kept him from fighting much longer.

I scanned the night and saw a Dark Fae shimmer before it

appeared to point at Dani. The leer he shot her was creepy as hell. "You're perfect for our amusements, little dragon. You don't know how to wield your powers. I'll enjoy taking you back to my place tonight, after we finish claiming this area as ours."

They thought they were going to take this area from us? Fat chance. Noah shifted into his wolf form and snapped his jaws around the Fae's leg before the idiot knew what was happening. Never threaten a wolf's fated one.

I jumped over the body of the elf I had killed, fighting the nausea that filled the back of my throat and jogged toward Lucas. The world seemed to slow around me, and I watched in horror, as a Dark Fae lifted a blade that was covered in strange markings. The weapon emitted a malevolent pulse of energy as the Dark Fae held it above Lucas's back. Lucas was fighting another Dark creature and didn't see this new threat. My screams filled the night as the Fae slammed the steel down into Lucas's wolf body. Luc's head lifted into the air but his howl never came. The man I was falling for collapsed to the ground in the middle of Jackson Square.

Dani shouted for me, but I never looked away from Lucas as his canine body disappeared. His fur fell away leaving tanned skin, at the same time his bones and muscles moved, cracked, and reshaped themselves. Lucas was an alpha. No one should be able to make him shift. Yet, whatever those symbols meant had forced the powerful man I loved to return to his human body.

Fear choked me as I shouted, letting my anger free, escaping with my voice. I conjured my witch fire at the same time and marched up to the Dark Fae that had stabbed Lucas. I grabbed hold of his maroon tunic and commanded my amber flames to consume the asshole. He writhed in agony for several seconds as I held him tight. Tears streamed down my cheeks when he turned to dust and my hands fell away.

FRENCH QUARTER FAE

The sounds of fighting echoed around me as I collapsed next to Lucas. My hand hovered above the weapon sticking out of him. I resisted the urge to pull it out. I recalled learning somewhere that a foreign object that's been stabbed into someone might be stopping them from bleeding to death

Noah and Dani rushed up to my side making me jump. I thought I was going to be attacked by another Dark Elf or one of his Fae brethren. I clasped Dani's hand and let her pull me to my feet as Noah bent to pick Lucas up from the ground. Noah was as naked as Lucas because they had shifted into their wolves.

Noah's current position gave me a view of his bare ass. I didn't care that he was naked as the day he was born for all to see. All my mind would focus on was Lucas and how he was seriously hurt. Noah was careful to leave the knife in Lucas's side. "We need to get him to Wynona. She's the only one that might be capable of healing him."

Dani had to push me to get me moving when Noah's naked backside raced past me carrying a bleeding and unconscious Lucas. Delphine joined us a second later. I turned and scanned the park, making sure we weren't leaving Kaitlyn to be killed. Hell, she might already be dead. I didn't see anything that happened after Lucas collapsed.

Kaitlyn jerked her chin in my direction. "I'll take care of the mundie memories," Kaitlyn called out as we followed Dani's mate.

Delphine grabbed my free hand while Dani held the other. "He's going to be alright, Lia. He's an alpha wolf shifter and one of the strongest paranormals alive," Phi said trying to make me feel better.

I wanted to believe her. I tried to ignore the fear that had taken over my mind. We'd been through so much already and made it through without many problems. He'd seen me brutally attacked and fighting for my life more often than I had him. No matter how hard I tried, I couldn't ignore the concern for his safety. I could tell myself he would live, but I couldn't push the niggle in the back of my mind that he might not be the same after this. That weapon had Dark Fae symbols and magic attached to it that made him shift. What exactly did it do to him? I prayed it hadn't killed his wolf. Lucas would be devastated if he lost his animal, his position, and his pack in one fell swoop.

CHAPTER 13

DANIELLE

Dakota pulled the scones out of the oven and placed them on the cooling rack. "We need to tell Phoebe about what's happening here. She's our Pleiades. While I don't understand exactly what that means, I know she's powerful and might be able to help us. We're in over our freaking heads on this one."

Dreya snorted as she scooped up a scone, put it on a plate, then handed it to Lia. She gave me one and then got one for herself while Cami and Kota served themselves. "We've been in shit up to our eyeballs ever since our magical DNA was unlocked," Dre said.

Dahlia pulled her phone from her back pocket and opened the FaceTime app. "You're both right. This time we have Fae threatening the French Quarter which places the mundies at risk and puts us at risk of exposure." Lia hit Phoebe's contact. "Hopefully, Phoebe can help."

I lifted a shoulder as the phone rang. "Or at least have some advice."

Phoebe and Stella's face appeared on the screen. Both looked like hell while Phoebe had dark circles under her eyes, bruises covering one side of her face and a strained smile barely lifting the corners of her mouth. "Hello. I can see I have most of the Twisted Sisters. What can I do for you? Hopefully, it's nothing Earth shattering. I have to get to the Underworld to deal with an emergency of my own."

My eyes practically bugged out of my skull when I heard her greeting. I lifted a hand into the air. "We shouldn't have called. We can figure this out."

Dahlia shook her head from side to side. "No, actually, we need information. It won't take long. The Dark Fae have joined forces with Marie Laveau and they're trying to take over the French Quarter."

"Can you tell us anything about these Fae?" Dre asked.

Kota held up a hand. "Specifically, how we can handle their invisibility. They attacked again last night and popped up out of nowhere."

Phoebe ran a hand down her face. "I have a little bit of time."

"Not much," Stella chimed in over her shoulder.

Phoebe inclined her head to her best friend. "Back up. How many are we talking? What are they doing?"

Dahlia briefly explained what had happened from the first attack, to Marie kidnapping us, and then the events last night. "We're hoping you can tell us how this is possible so we can prevent it. Along with how we can combat their invisibility. If supernaturals had been aware they were there sooner, we could have been called and avoided mundies being injured." We had discovered later that several people had been injured by Dark Fae. Dea was at work when she heard word that people were raving like lunatics about the monsters that had tried to kill them.

Stella moved beside Phoebe and was gaping at the screen by the time Dahlia finished explaining. The circles under Phoebe's eyes seemed to darken, as well. The Pleiades sipped a cup of coffee while she absorbed the information. Whatever was taking her to the Underworld was taking a toll on her.

Phoebe shook her head rapidly before she sighed. "My bestie in England, Fiona, told me about a spell she used when she was in the Eidothea, the Fae realm. She and Violet went there with Aislinn to help her have her baby. They ran across Dark Fae that had hidden encampments strategically placed to destroy the Light Fae. Anyway, they created a spell and potion to allow them to see through the enchantment they were using. It required the witches to combine their efforts with the Fae, so you will need to find someone to help with it."

Phoebe gave us the instructions that Fiona had shared with her. "I wish I could come out and help with this, but I have to travel to the Underworld right away. Not that I want to add to your plate, but I need your help now. This portal concerns me. We need to determine if there is a new gateway to Eidothea there. If that's the case, we will need to secure it and assign a guardian to ensure unauthorized Fae don't come through in New Orleans. Some species can reproduce rapidly and become a blight on an ecosystem. Connect with the Light Fae in your area and see what they know. I'm not sure when I will be back, so contact Fiona and let her know what you discover. As the current guardian for the Fae portal, she or her grandmother can take steps to get it under control. I'll let her know you'll be calling."

"Thank you for this. We will call the Light Fae here immediately in case there has been an open passage here for two weeks," Dre replied. "Thank you for your help. Stay safe and let us know if we can help you at all."

I had pulled my phone from my pocket and sent Drake a message asking him to have their representative come and talk with us. The thought of having these creatures flooding unchecked into our city made me sick to my stomach. By the time Lia ended the call with Phoebe, Drake let me know Cyran and Saida would be at Willowberry in half an hour.

"I messaged Drake about this," I told the others as I took a bite of my now cold scone. I preferred them hot but would never turn down one of Kota's cinnamon delicacies. "He's sending Cyran and Saida. One, or both, of them are their representatives. I figured whoever they voted for the council would be the best people to work with on this. They'll be here in a half an hour."

"I'd better make another batch of scones, then. What do you think was up with Phoebe? I'm glad we don't have her position. No damn way do I want to go to the Underworld." Kota shuddered as she grabbed a clean bowl.

Cami retrieved the ingredients from the pantry. "People shouldn't be able to visit the Underworld. You have to have certain blood in your veins in order to pass through the veil, if not you will be incinerated slowly. At least that's what I read in one of my mother's books. I'm sure Phoebe can go because she's mated to Aidoneus. Although, I do wonder if there is another, more sinister reason. She's been seriously injured recently."

I cocked my head to the side and watched as she helped Kota measure out the ingredients. "Do you think your powers are finally surfacing?"

Cami was resurrected accidentally by Phoebe months ago. Because she was a witch, she came back as a ghoul. Now that she had her soul back, she was a witch again but none of us knew when or if her specific talents would emerge. Every witch had a special ability that not all possessed.

Cami lifted a shoulder. "Not really. I can see illness and injury in people, but I can't do anything about it. I had to suppress my magic before, so I have no idea what I possessed when I lived before."

Lia clapped Cami on the shoulder and squeezed. "I don't know about that. I think some of your charisma can be attributed to a magical talent. You're the best tour guide I've ever had. Your knowledge and passion about the plantation are one reason you're so good. Yet, there's more. Who knows what it will become. Perhaps it's a precursor to some combination of empathy and healing. After all, your insight into a person is one reason you're so charismatic. You can tailor your stories to fit what each group will respond to best."

A lightbulb went off in my mind when Dahlia mentioned that. "You're right, Lia. You could go into politics, Cami."

Cami chuckled and shook her head. "No, thank you. I have no desire to work with men and women who allow themselves to be bought."

"When did you learn so much about politics?" Dre asked the question I was wondering.

A sardonic expression creased Cami's face making her look like she was born in this era. It warmed my heart to see how far she'd come since being brought back to life. Cami put the sheet of pastries in the oven. "The topics might be different today, but the people aren't."

"Good point," Lia conceded with a chuckle.

The doorbell chimed through the house making us jump. It was too early for the tours to start and everyone we knew used the back door. I had forgotten we were expecting visitors. I'd blame the memory lapse on getting older if I'd had my tall boy that morning. Yes, Pepsi was my version of coffee. It wasn't good for you, and I knew it, but it was one habit I couldn't break.

The five of us headed out of the kitchen to the front door. Two very different looking individuals stood on the covered porch. The woman was only a couple of inches taller than my five-foot-two and had the same extra fifteen pounds that I carried. She had long, red hair and piercing blue eyes and she was dressed in fancy slacks and a soft pink sweater with dress flats. The guy with her was tall, at least six feet with black hair and gray eyes. He had black jeans and a designer t-shirt on with boots.

Dre extended her hand. "Hi, I'm Dreya. The oldest of the Twisted Sisters and this is Dakota, Dahlia, Danielle, and Camilla. Please come in."

The guy lifted a hand. "Good morning. I'm Cyran and this is Saida. We're the Light Fae representatives for the Aegis council."

Lia gestured to the Ladies' Parlor. "Thank you for coming."

I took a seat on the sofa next to Kota while the Fae took the club chairs across from us. "I hope Drake told you why we needed to see you on such short notice."

Saida pursed her lips. "All he said was that it was an emergency requested by the Pleiades in Maine."

Cyran nodded. "Typically, we wouldn't respond to such a request without more, but Phoebe Dieudonné is good friends with the portal guardian and a trusted ally."

Getting a message like that had to be odd. I'd put as much detail into my text to Drake as possible to put them at ease. It would have been nice to have a warmer welcome from them. They were formal and aloof but not unfriendly. Lia explained what had been happening and what Phoebe had told us.

Cyran's hands clenched into fists on the arm rests. "We've been worried about the Dark Fae activity. We've patrolled each night and encountered a handful but haven't encountered full-scale attacks like that."

Saida lifted a hand in the air. "Not that they would engage if they saw us. They run when they see a Light Fae because we can fight their elemental magic."

"I bet they're hiding to avoid you seeing them and trying to stop them," I replied.

Cyran's forehead furrowed. "What do you mean they hide?"

Kota gasped and jumped to her feet startling our guests, Air whipped around the room making papers fly around. I assumed it was the Fae. Kota grimaced. "Sorry. I forgot about the scones. I'll be back. Would you like something to drink?"

The Fae shook their heads. Cami went to help Kota while Lia explained about the attacks and what Phoebe had said about the potion and spell. Cyran and Saida shared a look. "Fiona and her friends created this after they discovered Dark Fae hiding in our cities?"

Lia nodded. "That's what Phoebe told us."

Cyran looked like he'd been sucker punched. "It would have been nice if Fate had brought those women into our world sooner. Many lives could have been saved."

Saida smacked his shoulder. "That doesn't matter now. There's no changing the past." The Fae woman turned to face Dre, Lia, and me. "We'd be happy to work on these potions with you."

I stood up with a smile. "That's great to hear. Given the urgency in Phoebe's voice, there's no time like the present."

Kota and Cami were walking down the hall toward us at the same time we were leaving. I gestured to Dakota who was holding a platter of fresh scones. "Kota is a kitchen witch and our best potion maker, so she will be making the potion with you."

Dakota's face furrowed in confusion. "I am?"

Dre nodded and turned her around. "Yes, you are. We need to have this potion on hand."

Kota shrugged her shoulders and held out the tray as we left the house through the back door. "I'd be happy to make the potion. They're cinnamon chip, if you're hungry."

Cyran licked his lips and grabbed a pastry. "I already ate but these smell too good to resist." The guy moaned when he bit into the flaky, buttery goodness.

Saida watched him for two seconds before she too, gave in and took one. "These are delicious," she said around a mouthful.

I took a second scone thinking I should have brought my drink with me. We all ate in silence as we walked. The pixies came out of their mound as we passed and followed us to the magical kitchen. I sensed the questions Talewen and the others were holding back. We'd fill them in later. It was too much to go over again.

Inside the magic kitchen, Lia and Dre grabbed the fennel seed, ashwagandha root, calendula, hibiscus, and mugwort. Kota added some ground fennel to the cauldron she'd placed over the burner. "Now I stir it counterclockwise?"

I nodded. "Phoebe said we stir for a few seconds between each ingredient."

Talewen cleared her throat as Dakota worked. "What are we doing?"

I sighed as Lia did a brief recap with them. An herbal scent filled the room along with her words. It seemed like a long time until Kota's stirring slowed a bit. "Now what?"

Dre set her phone down. "Now the Fae runes need to be added to the mixture."

Saida accepted the spoon and turned it so she was holding the scoop. She stuck the straight end of the spoon in the mixture and carefully drew the first rune. Blue light flashed inside the container. I stood on tiptoe to see that it had turned the mixture a clear blue color. The liquid started to bubble and froth as the scent in the room intensified.

Saida didn't hesitate to draw the second rune. This time the light flashed purple, and the bubbles reached the middle of the large black pot. Purple smoke drifted up from the container, filling the room. My head swam and dizziness made me unsteady. I had to back up before it overwhelmed me.

Saida wavered like she was affected, too. Cyran steadied her and she drew the final rune. Teal light flashed and the potion bubbled to the top of the pot. Saida jerked her hand back. "I didn't want to destroy the rune," she explained.

The purple smoke was sucked back into the pot a second later. Next, teal mist hovered over the top. Kota stepped forward again and took the spoon. I lurched forward. "No, wait. Phoebe said they stopped stirring at this point."

Dakota's cheeks turned pink. "That's right. We need to write the details down in our grimoire."

Dre wiggled her phone from side to side. "I've already done that. I figured we'd leave it to Delphine to actually write since she'd been the one doing it thus far."

Lia flexed her fingers. "We wouldn't be able to read my chicken scratch."

I gasped and pointed to the pot. "It's clear. That means it's done" Surprisingly, it looked more like sludge as Kota scooped some up and poured them in the bottles Cami had set next to the cauldron.

"What do we do with these?" Cryan asked.

Dre picked up a bottle and looked at the contents. "According to Phoebe, you should drink it when you want to know if there are Fae hidden nearby. She didn't give us an exact time frame for how long it works. All she said was that it works for a short period of time."

Cyran inclined his head. "I will use it before I patrol tonight. Can we call on you if we need more?"

Dakota nodded as she finished bottling the potion. "Absolutely. I'd be happy to help anytime."

Cami pointed to the shelves. "We're low on some of the herbs. I'll put in an order for more."

I smiled at Cami and shifted gears to the other topic we needed to discuss. "Phoebe wanted us to discuss one more topic. Did you feel a portal opening about two weeks ago? Is there still a portal open here? I worry Marie might try to find a way to bring more here as we kill off her new allies. It would be good to know if you guys are aware if more arrive."

Saida tilted her head to the side and pursed her lips. "We felt a surge in energy, but we weren't able to determine what it was or what had caused it. It felt like it came from the French Quarter, so we assumed it was a new witch that lost control. It happens more often than you'd think."

Cyran nodded his head as he crossed his arms over his chest. The muscles of his biceps stretched the sleeves of his t-shirt tight around his flesh. "We didn't feel the pull of home if that helps. And we still don't so there isn't an active passage home in this city."

Dreya leaned forward as she clasped her hands on the table. "Is that something you would feel if a portal opened to your realm only briefly?"

"I believe that we would feel it regardless of the amount of time. We are sensitive to the power of where we came from. Many of our kind live in Cottlehill Wilds because that's where the portal home exists," Cyran replied. "They don't live there because the way home is close but because the magic that is unique to Eidothea is close enough to feel. Before Fiona, Aislinn, and Violet helped Sebastian and Argies get rid of the Evil Fae King, we were forced to flee. Life under Vodor was brutal."

Lia tapped the side of her water bottle. "This makes no sense and I'm not sure Marie can recreate the conditions to bring more Dark Fae here. The surge happened when we fought the loa. I suspect we might have used more of our Fae magic, and when it collided with the voodoo energy, it created a ripple that allowed the Fae to slip through."

I sighed and rubbed my temple where an ache was forming. "I can't sit here guessing anymore. It's giving me a headache. We can safely assume that, at a minimum, it will not be easy for Marie to try and bring additional Dark Fae here."

Saida gave me a sympathetic smile. "One thing to keep in mind is that the Dark Fae will not help her for long. They have their own agenda and will go to ground before they are all lost. And don't forget that many have lived here for years."

A ten-ton weight landed on my shoulders. It was too much. This was one more bad guy to add to a growing list. As a nurse in the neonatal intensive care unit for two decades, I was accustomed to my fair share of death and stress. This was a whole other ballgame. "The Aegis council can't be created fast enough."

CHAPTER 14

DAHLIA

"Why are we taking this?" Delphine asked as she tipped the bottle to the side. "We're just going to dinner, right? You aren't planning on going and looking for these evil entites are you?"

Kota gave Phi a droll look. "Have you forgotten our luck recently? No one wants any more shit than we've had lately, so just to be safe, my vote is to stay home for dinner tonight. We're playing with fire by leaving the plantation."

I grabbed my purse and headed to the back door, not wanting to miss this night out. "Lucas injured Marie. Thankfully he's an alpha shifter because shifting a few times had practically healed him completely. The same can't be said for Marie. Even if she lived, she can't be back in action yet. Between work and the cases that we've had in the magical world, we haven't had any sestra time in too long. Besides, this will be Cami's maiden voyage."

Cami choked as she listened to the conversation. "We

don't have to go. Phi might be right. The next Marie might be setting something up to get revenge."

Dani locked up after everyone was out of the back door. "The next Marie isn't ready to take over. The next generation doesn't have nearly as much power as her mother. Mom has been hoarding it for herself."

Dre pushed the seat back after Phi and Cami were in the back seat of my car. "I bet she can't even inherit the power until after her mom dies. I can't see Marie wanting to share any of it. She wouldn't have enough juice to pull off the shit that she has lately."

I nodded in agreement as I pulled out and headed toward the Jewel of the South restaurant. It was located on the outskirts of the Quarter, had the best cocktails, and was a place Cami asked to try after finding it online. It was great to see her blossom into a confident young woman.

Dea clapped her hands together. "Alright, sestras, it's time to set that crap aside and have some fun. Guess what I found, Dani. Remember that time we went dune hang gliding?" Dea devolved into a fit of laughter that soon had the entire car in hysterics, even Cami.

Dani was waving a hand in front of her face as she laughed so hard. "Oh my God. That guy was like what the hell is wrong with this lady?"

Dea pulled out her phone and pushed play. All I heard was a man make a pffft noise. I wracked my brain to recall what video they were watching as Dea began devolved into a fit of giggles.

It was Cami that shed some light on it for me. "You stopped right as you were supposed to start gliding. What happened?"

Dani was too busy laughing to respond for several seconds. "I have no idea."

Dea teased Dani about the situation while the others

shared funny stories of their own. My heart lightened as I drove and listened to them. This was how it usually was when we were all together. Sharing fun experiences while everyone chuckled. It was fun and carefree. This was one thing I missed the most now. The paranormal cases had taken over and we didn't have enough of these moments.

Sure, we still laughed and had fun, but it wasn't the same as it used to be. I almost regretted taking the potion with us on this little outing. We needed an uncomplicated evening filled with good food and even better company. I contemplated telling everyone not to drink their potions. Reality intruded as I parked in a spot a few blocks away from the restaurant. We couldn't deny the fact that we were targets. And the last thing we wanted was to be blindsided.

I grabbed my bottle from my purse and held it up. "Bottom's up, sestras." Uncorking the vial, I tipped it back and swallowed the thick potion. My mouth objected to the bitter concoction and I started coughing along with the rest of the people in the car. The stuff coated my tongue and the back of my throat.

Kota shook her head from side to side and covered her mouth. "There has to be a way to make that taste better." The others spilled out of the vehicle.

Phi wiped her mouth with the back of her hand. "We will need to ask Kaitlyn if changing anything will alter the magic. Every plant has power."

Dea threaded her arm through Dani's and started down the block to the restaurant. "I'm going to get the swamp water. That drink is delicious."

Dani oohed in response. "You're determined to relive our trip to Southport, aren't you? Do you think they'll have it here?"

Dre pushed her head between Dea and Dani's as they walked. "Every city in the south has a version of swamp water. I prefer the one with vodka, Midori, pineapple juice, and Sprite."

A couple walking on the other side of the street crossed and headed right for us. My heart started racing while I ran through the best offensive spells to use. Moving closer to Dre, Dani, and Dea, I reached back and pulled Phi and Cami to me. Kota plastered herself to Cami's side. Thoughts of Dani's dragon filled my head when I felt heat coming off of her like a furnace set to high.

"It's lucky that we ran into you tonight." The male voice was familiar. Relief washed through me as they passed under the streetlight. It was Cyran and Saida.

Dre walked out from behind Dea and Dani. "We are heading to dinner." I appreciated that she didn't leave room for discussion. She was not about to let them hijack our night.

Cyran dipped his head. "You'll want to put that off and drink that potion we made. We're close to discovering the location of where Laveau pulled the Dark Fae through."

"We also sense a concentration of energy nearby. It could be where they're hiding out," Saida added.

Dani sighed and pinched the bridge of her nose. "I knew taking that potion was asking the Universe to intrude on our evening. Let's go kick some Fae ass."

I chuckled, letting go of the last of the tension making me rigid. "We'll make some swamp water when we get back. I have a feeling we're going to need it after tonight."

Kota scowled at our new Fae friends. "We're grabbing something to eat, too. I'm not doing this without food."

"I don't know, sestra, it might make you more lethal if you're hungry," Phi teased.

I gestured in the opposite direction from where we were heading. "Is the energy in that direction?"

Saida shook her head from side to side. "Nope. It's where

we think Laveau pulled the Dark Fae through." She turned around and we all started walking down the middle of the street.

We were on the outskirts of the Quarter which meant there was wasn't much vehicular or pedestrian traffic. Still, it wasn't long before the honk of a horn forced our large group onto the sidewalk. We marched like soldiers doing basic training for a few seconds. Unlike in the military, our group was silent. All that could be heard were our footsteps and the occasional car.

Cami cleared her throat. The sound was loud compared to the ambient noise around us. "If you can sense the magic lingering in this spot does that mean Marie, or the others, can open it and bring more through?"

Cyran lifted one shoulder. "Fae aren't portal builders. A Shakleton witch created the one to Eidothea a long time ago. However, seeing what we accomplished by combining our powers, I have no idea what is possible."

Saida gasped and pointed to a dark space between two houses. I assumed she was pointing out the spot where the Dark Fae came through, because I didn't see anything out of the ordinary, in the ten feet separating the residences. With nothing visible to clue me in, I opened my senses and searched for an energy signature. It took a few seconds before I felt it. It was like the torn corner of a curtain was blowing in the breeze.

Once identified, I could see that it was a small slit in the fabric of the veil. "Can you seal that off?"

Cyran and Saida moved closer. Cyran lifted a finger that ignited like a lighter. He used the tip to draw a rune in the air about three and a half feet off the ground. Orange sparks shot out from the symbol, making Cyran and Saida duck. My sisters and I had remained on the sidewalk. I scanned the front doors lining the street, praying no one came outside.

"Let's try to dispel it together," Saida suggested.

I hurried forward then stopped short when I got a better view of the space and was able to see a bright green line bisecting the space directly in front of Cyran. "How the hell can I see this?"

Phi was right beside me. "It's the potion, Lia. It's allowing us to see through what the Dark Fae were trying to hide. I bet money they did that so Marie could use it again."

That's what I was thinking, too. And it was the last thing we needed to allow. "We should combine efforts to close this rift completely."

Dre nodded and grabbed hands with Cami and Kota. "I was just thinking the same thing. What's the best spell for us to use? *Prope?*"

Dani pursed her lips and joined hands with Phi and Dea while I grabbed hold of Dea. "That's as good as any because the words give voice to our intent." Her comment made me wonder if we could make up words to use for spells. I'd ask Kaitlyn one day.

Keeping my eyes trained on the green crack through the air, I pictured the green being sucked through a massive straw in the sky and taking the hum of energy I could feel with it. I made sure to picture the cool evening breeze blowing through the area and dissipating any molecules of power that were left behind so no one could use them to open a rift to Eidothea again.

Saida and Cyran drew runes in fire. Dre signaled us and the seven of us chanted our spell to seal the tear. Electricity traveled through us and crackled through the air and snaked out to the ripple in front of us. A loud roar filled the space making the seven of us flinch. I bet we looked like we were doing the wave as we moved gently together.

Cyran and Saida turned smiles to us. "Seems as if Fiona

and her friends started a trend. Word will spread fast about how well witches and Fae can work together."

Kota pretended to fluff the side of her hair. "We're definitely bitches you want to know. Now, let's grab a beignet and see if we can find that hideout."

Cyran took us on a different street from the one we came down. Less than five feet away from the rift we ran across a voodoo supply shop. We barely made it past the store when Delphine started shaking and grabbed ahold of Dani and Dre. They held her. "It's happening." Her voice changed pitch and tone then. "The Queen hangs in the balance. Push her to the right and death will follow. Pull her to the left and a new power will be set free."

"Boy those are nothing like your smell-o-visions, Lia," Kota commented.

I smirked at her. Phi's new power was nothing like what happened to me. "We shouldn't hang around here for long. I don't like lingering close to anything having to do with that woman."

Dani shuddered as Dre brought Phi closer to her side. "It makes me twitchy."

"I can walk," Phi croaked then cleared her throat. "It's disorienting but that talisman warned me before it happened but not by much."

Dea shot Phi a smile. "It's gives you more than you had before. And you will be able to extend it beyond that. You kicked cancer's ass. This will be nothing compared to that battle."

Phi straightened and held her head high. "You're right. There's hope. And the best part is that I might be able to cut my leave short," Phi agreed as we walked. "What did I say this time?"

I was only half listening as Dea told her what she'd said because I couldn't shake the feeling that someone was

FRENCH QUARTER FAE

watching us. I'm fairly certain it was my imagination running wild after Phi having the premonition near one of Marie's shops. Especially since something triggered her vision. My visions were activated by a scent. Perhaps the energy around Marie's shop made Phi get hers.

I scanned the street behind us before we turned another corner but couldn't locate the reason it felt like we were being watched. Kota pointed to a café, then she and Dani went up to get some beignets to hold us over until we could grab dinner. I couldn't shake the feeling there was someone following us.

Phi rubbed her arms as she glanced around, as vigilant as me. "We should have gone down for that salted caramel ice cream."

I groaned as I recalled the small caramel filled chocolate bits inside the ice cream. "That's a much better idea for dinner."

One of Cami's eyebrows lifted. "Ice cream is the best invention since I was born. That combination sounds delicious. Can we get some on our way home?"

Cyran gestured to the black and white sign for the shop that sold the creamy treat. "Do you want me to grab you some while we wait."

We all nodded our heads. We hadn't even opened our mouths to reply when the guy raced away. Saida chuckled at our shocked expressions. "He used your desire as an excuse. It's his favorite, as well."

"I fully support using any means necessary to obtain ice cream," I laughed.

Kota and Dani were back carrying white paper bags. Dre clapped them on the back and told them where Cyran went. Their eyes went wide as grins spread across their faces. Kota opened a bag and tore of a small piece of a beignet then popped it in her mouth. "I'm going to get a stomachache from eating all this sugar."

Phi nodded her head as we started walking. "I'll need real food soon."

Saida pointed to a smaller street on our right. "The area where we felt the concentration of energy is down that way."

Cyran exited the ice cream store right before we reached it. He handed out spoons and passed four pints of ice cream between us. "I figured we could share."

Dani snorted. "I'll share my beignets and take your pint."

I opened my ice cream and crossed the street. This late at night, the side street wasn't busy with tourists because there weren't any restaurants or bars. The few souvenir shops were closed. I scooped creamy goodness into my mouth and savored the sweet treat.

We were all busy eating and not paying attention when creatures descended on us. A small red demon landed on my head making me throw my pint in the air. Screams filled the air as more of the imps jumped on us.

"Is it just demons? Do you see any Dark Fae? I don't," Kota shouted. "Did the potion stop working?"

"I don't think Fae are involved," Dani replied.

Phi flared her hands, freezing two of them while another took the bags from Dani and Kota. They took the fried dough from the bags and tossed powdered sugar everywhere. I kicked out at one trying to grab my purse. Phi froze that imp, too. But her powers didn't last long, it just slowed them down. It became immediately clear that they weren't there to harm us.

Cyran snarled and batted one into the side of a building. "Fucking imps. Apparently, they thrive on salted caramel ice cream and chaos." There were about half a dozen surrounding us. Most were eating the frozen treat while the others were having fights with the powdered sugar.

The hair on my neck stood on end as I turned to walk away from the mischievous creatures. They weren't worth fighting. Four massive beasts moved from the shadows and blocked our path. The newcomers stood eight feet tall, had charcoal colored skin, with three rows of horns on their heads and razor-sharp fangs.

Dre pointed at a brick in the alley and sent it sailing toward one of the monsters. Cyran was a flurry of fists and feet. Kota conjured a machete and handed one to me before she had another in her hand. I pulled my hand back and swung my sword at one of the beasts. My blade sliced through its side right as a guy jumped from the roof to our left.

Cami yelped and jumped back when Xinar landed in front of her. He was a good-looking Asian man with black hair and brown eyes. He was tall and wearing a tailored suit that fit his muscular build very well. What was a businessman doing jumping off of roofs?

Xinar had two short swords in his hands and sliced through the demon that was about to attack Cami. His mere presence frightened the demons. The imps took off first. The three remaining massive demons didn't get very far. Cyran finished off the creature he was fighting while our savior took out the last two. Once all the demons were dead, he pressed some kind of a coin to their dead bodies making them disappear.

Xinar extended his hand to Cami first and shook her hand. I swear he gave her a look of appreciation. Was he a playboy? He'd been flirty with Phi last time. "I'm Xinar, a UIS Agent and here to help with the increased demonic activity."

"I'm Camilla. I'm, I, uh live at Willowberry with the Smith sisters." Cami blushed and lowered her head.

I smiled at Xinar. "Thanks for coming to the rescue. You

said activity has gotten worse. Did Marie Laveau use the tear in the veil to pull demons through, as well?"

Xinar brushed his hands down his suit jacket. The guy was immaculate. Not a hair out of place. How did he fight in that suit and not get it dirty? "I don't think it was Marie. She stays within her pantheon of gods. The loa would be pissed if she enlisted demons in her machinations. My guess is that some Tainted witches used the flux of power that I felt a couple of weeks ago at your parade. It was powerful enough to allow them to work around the Hellmouth because it's not close to here."

Dre explained what we were doing in the Quarter, the Fae attacks, what had happened when Marie kidnapped Dani and I, and about the Aegis council creation. "It seems fitting that you become part of the group since you are now placed here. Especially since I assume you'll want to be contacted when demons are located."

Xinar's eyebrows both went up to his hairline. "You six are responsible for the best changes in the magical world. Before Aidon mated Phoebe, I assumed it was best if UIS agents remained separate from others. Now, I see the benefit of having close working relationships. It makes everyone safer."

I was glad Dre thought of this. I was frazzled from the encounter with demons. The remaining hex in my system was to blame for me being in less than top shape. Particularly when this fight hadn't been much of one for us, thanks to Xinar. "In the meantime, will you keep your eyes peeled for Marie's mambos and Dark Fae? Marie's going to be pissed when she recovers, and it would be nice to get a leg up on her."

Xinar inclined his head. "I'd be happy to keep my eyes peeled and let you know if I find anything."

We thanked him and went our separate ways. It didn't

take long before Dani stopped on the corner of Bourbon and Anne, holding up her hands. "We should call it a night. We can patrol another time. We have an anniversary party to prepare for and we all need food. We lost our ice cream and beignets, and I have no more energy."

Kota nodded her head in agreement. "The demons probably made the Dark Fae hide, but you two can continue."

I chuckled at the look of exasperation on Cyran's face and clapped him on the shoulder. "It's best if we come back to this another time. Call us if you find anything. Preferably not tonight."

Cyran and Saida agreed to call it a night and we went our separate ways. Our allies expanded by leaps and bounds lately. I just hoped that didn't mean our paranormal case load would do the same. I enjoyed dealing with paranormal situations. While I wanted to help stop the Dark Fae from outing the existence of the magical world, I wasn't so sure I wanted to help with this insurgence of demons, too. With the arrival of Xinar, I didn't feel as much pressure to take it on. With his help, hopefully, we will locate the Dark Fae's hide-out and stop them.

CHAPTER 15

DAHLIA

I watched Phi roll up the scroll on which she had written the official agreement as Lucas, Cyran, Kaitlyn and Albar developed the wording. Phi had taken notes as the group threw out suggestions before she wrote out the final document. She clutched it tightly in her hands, obviously as nervous as I was.

My stomach jumped like a can of jumping beans as I sat at the large table in Kaitlyn's house. She was centrally located in the Garden District and agreed to host the first meeting. Pack lands were too far outside of town to be convenient. Not to mention Lucas had no desire to welcome the head vampire onto his property.

Lucas ran his thumb over the back of my hand as he spoke with Kaitlyn, Cyran, and Viktor, the new leader of the vamps in town. We had all been shocked when the vampire arrived. "We need a building where we can hold these meetings so no one's residence is indisposed." Lucas and I had discussed this earlier, and it had nothing to do with being a burden but with the desire to have a spot that was neutral and allowed for represented species to go and report concerns.

Viktor tugged on the lapel of his black suit jacket. "Preferably one that's easily concealed by a spell that won't draw attention if people come and go from it. Your home isn't exactly friendly, Kaitlyn. I can feel the hostility."

Kaitlyn smiled sweetly at Viktor. "You've always had pristine senses, Viktor. We all appreciate you representing the vampires. Understand this council is being created to prevent anyone from gaining too much power over the others. Everyone will be expected to follow the rules that are established."

Someone knocked on the door interrupting the conversation. Kaitlyn got up to answer it and returned with Xinar. Viktor stiffened in his seat and seemed to lose even more color from his already pale face. I got up and shook Xinar's hand. "Thanks for coming. It's important that you're part of this." I introduced Xinar to the others. The representative for the elves, demons, djinn, gargoyles, and necromancers arrived shortly after.

I sat next to Lucas with my sisters positioned around me. Dre and Kota were at the table with the rest of us behind her to save seats up close for others. There were two empty chairs between Xinar and Kaitlyn. I had insisted we keep them open for the voodoo segment and the Dark Fae. Not that I necessarily wanted them to be a part of this council. However, I knew that having their agreement and involvement would make it harder for them to continue with their bullshit.

Keryth Hernan, the rep for the elves, cleared his throat and gestured to us. "Why are there so many witches on the council. That's not an equal start to this historic process."

Kaitlyn took a deep breath and forced a smile on her face. "The Smith sisters are different from anyone present. They have characteristics of just about every paranormal species which makes them a unique unit. They don't have a dog in the game and are as close to neutral as you can get."

Viktor slammed his hands on the table. "That's not true. They are enemies with Marie Laveau who is conspicuously absent from the table."

Dre snarled at the vampire. "That's because she is busy recovering from a fatal wound after kidnapping my sisters and trying to sacrifice them to her loa. She's also partnered with the Dark Fae who have their own twisted plans for our city."

Xinar lifted a hand. "I assume there are seats reserved for both the Dark Fae and voodoo at this table. I was told the Aegis council is representative of all creatures in the area. As I understand it, they haven't been located to receive their invitations."

Shayla, an attractive woman that oozed sexuality tossed her long auburn hair over her shoulder. She was the elected demon rep. "We're off topic. The Twisted Sisters come as a group. I don't mind as long as they don't have any more pull than the rest of us."

Lucas snorted. "No one should mind given the problems they've continually solved for our city. We need, and want, them on our side. They're proving to be a powerful bunch with unique abilities that will make our lives better."

Viktor glared at Lucas. "As a mate to one of them, you're biased."

Kaveh cleared his throat and spoke up for the first time. He'd been staring at Kaitlyn the entire time. "That very well might be the case, but there is no denying the impact the Twisted Sisters have had on our world. And it has been for the better. It's only those doing things they know they shouldn't that aren't happy with them."

Kaitlyn stood up. "I agree. Now, we need to address important issues, not discus trivial matters. The sisters work together and represent one seat. They might not all be present at every meeting. They aren't what we need to talk about. We need to establish how this council will work."

The front door banged open and my heart dropped. Marie Laveau stood in the entrance with a tall, lithe man with shoulder length blonde hair tied at the nape of his neck. His hazel eyes were full of malice as he scanned the room. "You were going to exclude me from this Aegis Council?" The Dark Fae asked.

Kaitlyn kept her composure and gestured to the empty chairs. "Not at all which is why you're here. As you can see your seat is waiting. As is the one for your Dark Fae companion."

Marie's jaw clenched as she moved with deliberation through the house and to the open chair. Her gaze stuttered on Kaveh. She was surprised to see the djinn amidst the gathering. "What have the abominations suggested this time?"

Albar growled, the sound was like boulders rolling down a hill because he was in his stone gargoyle form rather than his human one. "The paranormals of this city are taking back their power. You are no longer the unofficial leader of the French Quarter. And you will no longer exploit others."

"By sitting at this table, you are agreeing to a violence free discussion about establishing the rules for this council," Kaveh informed Marie and her friend.

"Remzyn and I are aware of what you're trying to do. The first order of business I would like discussed is the acknowledgement of our claim to certain sections of the city. We will not permit our land to be taken from us," Marie declared.

That sparked arguments from everyone sitting at the table. I sat back with my sisters as I watched them speak over one another while trying to be heard. Phi leaned toward me. "How am I supposed to write all of this down?"

I shook my head while keeping my eyes on Marie. She was glaring at me as she spoke. "You only need to document what everyone agrees upon."

Cyran put two fingers into his mouth and let out a piercing whistle. It shut down all conversations. "This bickering will get us nowhere. We need to get down the basic rules for the council. I'll go first. The first thing we need to agree to is to leave each group to live as they need without interference as long as it doesn't involve murder or exposure of our existence. As the elected leaders, we will be responsible for policing our people."

"I'd add that we can all give an opinion on an issue that someone brings to this council. I suspect others will bring their issues to us to get help resolving them. And when that happens, we all can give our input but it will be up to the leader to enforce what is decided on. Also, when something is suggested in these meetings, we take a vote and say yes or no without further comment. If we get into lengthy discussions about each rule, we will be here for a month," Lucas added. "I'm in favor of Albar's suggestion that each faction leader make specific additions that apply to their people. And that the entire council must weigh in when someone breaches the agreement."

Kaitlyn lifted a hand. "I am, too."

Marie took over and asked the remaining individuals what they thought. After everyone agreed, Phi wrote the details on the parchment scroll. Cyran suggested we add a guarantee of safe travel to and from meetings while Tempe suggested that no one is allowed to siphon power from another. Everyone agreed to those terms and Phi documented it.

Dre put forth that there would be no violence or aggression during meetings and no overt attacks on a fellow leader. Kota added that the council members would discourage their people from attacking others. There was some discussion about these topics and Marie, of course objected outright. When Viktor pointed out that we needed to feel secure that no one would be walking into a trap by coming to a meeting, Marie finally agreed to those terms.

Shayla, the demon leader talked about each leader developing a written document of the basic rules each group abides to so the council has a baseline to make a determination about complaints. Most rules would be universal and apply to everyone. However, each species required specialized items based on their needs. Shifters had different restraints than witches.

The last issue that was talked about was where to hold these meetings. It was Marie that said she would donate money so we could purchase a place designed for the council like Viktor suggested. The others agreed forcing the six of us to, as well. I had no idea how we were going to come up with the money, but we couldn't refuse. After all, this was my idea in the first place.

Marie lifted her chin into the air and pinned each person with her gaze. I felt the power she was sending out at us. It made me nauseous. "This council is wonderful, but we need a leader for it. Of course, it should be me since this is my city."

Kaveh laughed mirthlessly. "That's counter-productive considering you're the reason we needed to form this council in the first place. If anyone should lead this group it should be Dahlia or Dreya."

The djinn's comment made my heart race and started yet another round of arguments. Kaitlyn clapped her hands together while Kaveh muttered something that stopped all talking. The head witch took a deep breath and started choking. I looked around wondering what was happening when I saw Marie drawing symbols on the table in front of her in blood. She dipped her finger in a container and wrote another one. Her magic slithered around us and started tightening around my chest making it hard to breathe.

"Together," Kaveh croaked. I nodded even though he was looking at Kaitlyn. I linked hands with Dani and Phi. Within seconds, everyone in the room had clasped hands and Kaveh was muttering a counter spell. It took several seconds where energy was drained from me before Marie cried out and crumpled. Remzyn caught her and held her up.

"That's precisely the kind of shit that cannot happen in this council," I growled. "You will not beat us, Marie. We have joined together to maintain our sovereignty. Your days of subjugating the paranormals of New Orleans are over."

Kaitlyn nodded her head. "Dahlia is right. You will no longer be able to force us to comply with your terms. Every supernatural being living here is done doing what you want. You've lost your ability to cow us through fear. You no longer have power over us."

Kaveh leaned forward with his hands clasped. "If you want to remain here, you must enter into a binding agreement. It's one that all of us must abide by. Only those who agree will be permitted to remain in the area. The voodoo nation can elect a new leader should you chose not to agree."

I held my breath as I watched Marie Laveau scowl at the entire room. Her Dark Fae ally crackled with energy and was poised to respond at a moment's notice. The tension in the air was enough to make my stomach ache. It seemed as if Marie was going to refuse to agree to the basic terms already established. What was going to happen if she did that?

Her rage over losing her foothold was evident. I could see

the wheels turning in her mind. I imagined she was looking for a way she could manipulate this to go in her favor. Fortunately for the rest of us, the rules already suggested made Marie's total domination impossible.

After several tense minutes, Marie finally dipped her head. "I'll agree to the terms. However, these rules do not apply to previous grievances I have with certain individuals." My heart jumped into my throat with her obvious threat to my sisters and me. "Plan on adopting my suggestions at the next council meeting. I was indisposed and unable to prepare better thanks to a certain alpha attack. Which I trust will not happen again given these new rules."

Lucas leaned across the table and snarled. "You can guarantee I'll rip your head off of your shoulders if you go after my mate again. Everyone on the council is aware that falls under your previous grievances."

Remzyn's fingers sparked with flames as his eyes bore into Lucas. "You do not speak to the Queen this way. All of you are lucky she graces you with her presence. She has a legitimate claim." I had to fight the urge to burn the guy to ashes with my witch fire for his aggression toward Lucas.

Albar, who had been in his gargoyle form throughout the evening lifted a stone arm and pointed at Remzyn. "That's not how this works. All previous grievances are voided. Marie agreed not to take overt action against another leader. All of the Twisted Sisters are leaders of their kind."

Marie snorted and held up her hand. "That's fine. Although, I find it funny how you are classifying them since they don't have a kind. They're weak mixtures of too many species to have any real power. It's all diluted."

"Enough. We will not argue about this. Your vendetta is over, Marie. As is your threat to the Quarter." Kaitlyn tapped the table twice giving Kota the signal to conjure the ceremonial dagger they'd talked about previously. Kota got up and lifted her hand, palm up and smiled at everyone as she crossed to Kaitlyn. An ornate fountain pen and dagger appeared on her palm as she moved. She had everyone's attention then. Surprisingly, Viktor had an appreciative look in his eyes,

Dakota handed the dagger to Kaitlyn and placed the pen beside her. Phi handed the scroll to Lucas who slid it across to Kaitlyn. The formal council agreement was written on the paper. They would add addendums with further agreed upon changes. The head witch set the knife aside and held her hand out to Cyran who clasped it. Together they enchanted the agreement.

Kaitlyn signed the agreement with the pen then nicked her finger and pressed her blood beside her name. Red light burst from the blood as tiny white electricity traveled over the paper and up Kaitlyn's arm. Cyran was next. One by one each of the representatives signed. Remzyn, the Dark Fae representative paused for a second before he too, signed the agreement. The reaction was dimmer than the others had been. My gut twisted in knots as I prayed that he hadn't found a way around the magical binding. The light was black when Marie signed making everyone gasp.

Kaitlyn smirked at the Queen of Voodoo. "You're magically bound by this agreement, regardless of your intent."

The look Marie shot the head witch could have killed. I'm certain Marie meant for her exit to be far more dramatic than the slow exit she managed with the help of Remzyn. There was a certain satisfaction seeing that she needed help. She wasn't in as good of shape as she wanted us to believe.

CHAPTER 16

DANIELLE

The theme song for Harry Potter echoed through the kitchen. Who the hell was calling me this late at night? My heart skipped a beat when I saw Saida's name on the caller ID. I raced to the hall and called out to Lia before pressing the green button to accept the call.

"Dani, we need your help. Something's happened." Saida's voice was strained and off. It sent goosebumps all over my arms.

Phi and Lia came running into the kitchen with Lucas and Noah behind them. I put the call on speaker. "What happened, Saida? What's wrong?"

A deep inhale echoed through the small speaker. "I've been weakened. I was out patrolling with Cyran after the council meeting and was barely able to light the logs in my fireplace. I tried filling my bathtub and couldn't add more than a few gallons before I had to stop."

Noah placed his hand on my shoulder. "Did you

encounter any Dark Fae during your patrol?"

"Not one. I saw some imps jumping across balconies and texted Xinar about where he could find them," Cyran replied.

Lucas's confused expression echoed Noah's. "It sounds magical in nature. Did you have contact with anyone at all?"

"Aside from Cyran, the only other person I spoke to was Tiffany who is another Light Fae. I'm afraid to involve Cyran in case it's something contagious, so I'm hoping you can help." Saida sounded desperate. And frightened. I imagined she didn't experience stuff like this very often.

Noah inclined his head and gave me a sympathetic smile knowing I didn't want to leave the house again. "Give us your route so we can retrace your steps and find out if there are any clues left behind."

I held up a finger even though Saida couldn't see me. "Is there anyone else that's been affected like you?"

"I have no idea. I'll call around and see if anyone else is weakened," Saida offered.

I nodded my head to Phi and Lia, as well as Saida. "Alright. Text your route and call whoever you can. We will check in with you in a bit."

Saida thanked us and said goodbye. Marie and the Dark Fae were behind this. I just knew it. The five of us agreed to go to downtown and search through the streets Saida had walked. Lucas drove us there in his truck and parked in Ricky's garage. We took the potion then headed toward Decatur.

We were approaching Café DuMonde when Dahlia grunted and her eyes rolled back in her head. Lucas caught her and we moved closer to the buildings and out of foot traffic. "I hope this vision gives us answers," Lucas said as he ran a hand down Lia's platinum blonde hair.

The roots were growing out. I'd need to touch it up soon. "And I hope it wasn't the smell of beignets that triggered this or she will be pissed." Knowing Lia, she would deny herself the sugary treat to avoid having another vision. Or she would forever connect the vision to the fried dough and if she witnessed a horrific murder then she wouldn't be able to ever eat them again. Either way, she would be denied one of her favorite desserts.

It wasn't long before Lia shook her head and laid it on Lucas's shoulder. "I'd like to say that was helpful, but it wasn't. I saw us getting a pedicure and talking to a woman about the people working for her. It wasn't much and seemed to have nothing to do with this."

A whine fought to get out of my throat. Instead, I bit it back and pulled out my cell phone to call Saida while we walked. I scanned our surroundings as we turned down a side street. "Dani. Did you find something?"

I sighed at what my eagerness caused. I should be more patient. "Not yet. I was curious if anyone else is experiencing the same symptoms."

"Actually, yeah. Ella, Natalie and Fifi are weak, as well. Cyran is fine, though."

My eyes popped open and I yanked Noah's sleeve. The others stopped with me. "Then we aren't likely to find anything on our route. Let's shift gears. I'd like to come visit you four. I can use my psychometric powers on your personal belongings. Can they be at your place in fifteen? You live on Royal Street, right?"

"Yeah, I'm in the gray house with maroon shutters. They will all be here before you arrive. Thanks, Dani. I appreciate the help," Saida replied before she hung up.

I twined my gloveless fingers with Noah's. "She knows of three others but Cyran wasn't affected, so I doubt we will find anything on their route. We need to go to Saida's place."

Lia zipped her jacket up as a cold breeze gusted around us. "That's smart, especially since there are others that weren't out patrolling with them. I still want to keep an eye out for the Dark Fae and their lair. Cyran believes it's somewhere in the Quarter."

Phi pointed to an empty building as we walked. "That's a great location for the council. It's centrally located and doesn't have lofts above it which will make it easier to hide magically."

Lia pursed her lips. "It would be nice if we could create a portal of sorts from a location here to a place far from mundies. I hate that we will be drawing more paranormals to an area rife with humans that could expose us."

Lucas ran a finger over her cheek. "That's not necessary. We will make sure the mundies aren't hurt or exposed. This is a good location, but it would be better to pick a place on the other end of the Quarter. There are fewer tourists and a simple aversion ward will suffice to keep it hidden."

Noah and Lucas talked about places they thought would fit the bill as we walked. Honestly, it didn't matter to me, as long as we didn't have to put in too much money. We were doing great right now, but couldn't afford to contribute much.

Before long, we arrived at Saida's house and knocked on the maroon door. The Light Fae woman opened up and pulled me inside. "I had them bring their purses. I wasn't sure what you would need but it's the one thing they take everywhere with them."

My mind objected to my plan of touching countless items to see if I could learn what had happened to them. Noah stuck by my side and sat next to me on the loveseat. Phi and Lia sat on the couch while Saida and her friends hovered nearby. Saida gestured to a woman, as tall and slender as her, with dark brown hair that had blonde highlights. "This is Ella. And that is Fifi," she pointed to the woman with black hair and blue eyes. Her finger moved to the third woman who had brown hair and hazel eyes. "And this is Natalie. We haven't had a chance to call anyone else, yet, but we will continue to ask around. We can't have more Fae weakened like this when our enemy is among us."

Fifi nodded her head up and down rapidly. "It has got to be them that is making us this way. They hate what we represent and want to eliminate us."

"It's nice to meet you. We want to stop this, too, and will keep looking for answers." I extended my hand in Saida's direction. "I'll start with your bag."

Saida handed me a brown leather purse that looked handmade. It was soft and very well crafted. The hum of memories clung to the material before I even touched the fabric. I forced my mind to remain above them so I didn't get sucked in. It took effort, but I scanned the surface of them looking for anything out of place. I didn't need to know what she was thinking when she went to Final Swallow the night before last. There was a memory from a guy that bumped into Saida as an attempt to get her to talk to him.

Deciding there was nothing more there, I opened the top and dumped the contents onto the counter. I did a quick scan feeling for foreign power before I searched the surfaces of the memories. It took longer than I liked to sort through the items. A blush crept over my face when I saw Saida responding to a guy hitting on her. Shaking off the flood of input that hit me over the past ten minutes, I scooped the stuff up and put it back inside the bag. "Sorry for making a mess of your handbag. Let me try Fifi's next." I inhaled trying to shake off the fatigue and disorientation that using my powers caused.

Saida smiled at me, and it highlighted the dark circles underneath her eyes. "No worries. I appreciate your help."

My breath caught when I took the pink canvas bag from Fifi. There was a memory of her arguing with a co-worker about a theft. Fifi's disapproval was glaringly obvious. I wished her luck with that situation, then clamped my mouth shut when she gaped at me. "I can't help what I see."

Fifi clasped her hands in front of her torso. "I didn't realize you would see so much. My boss put me in a horrid position that I'm not sure how to handle."

I smiled at the Fae woman. "I can't tell you what to do but I will say that you have to follow your gut and stick to your principles. If you compromise your integrity, it will haunt you for a long time. You have to love who looks back at you in the mirror or no one else will."

"That's the reminder I needed. You're a rockstar in my mind even if you don't find anything else," Fifi said.

I chuckled and resumed my search. It was daunting to keep myself above the memories and not let them pull me into a reverie where I became Fifi and felt and experienced what she did. Fifi was far more emotional than Saida. She was what I'd call a touchy-feely person.

My shoulders were sagging by the time I finished with Fifi's stuff. Noah put her belongings back and grabbed Ella's bag. My head started pounding as I worked through her wallet, lipstick and other belongings. Bile filled the back of my throat when I started on Natalie's purse. I sat back with a sigh when I finished all of them. "Dammit. I found nothing. I'm sorry."

Phi reached over and squeezed my hand. "Don't feel bad, sestra. I know you're hurting, but what if you try touching their shoes and arms before we find another avenue to investigate? Those are the two places on a person that come in contact most often with foreign objects."

I nodded. "Good idea. At least then we will know we tried everything." My hand weighed a hundred pounds as I tried to lift it and reach for Saida's arm. She was perched on the coffee table.

FRENCH QUARTER FAE

There was a tingle of energy when my hand passed several feet over her foot. I gasped and lurched forward, reaching for her shoe. Noah caught me and kept me from falling off of the sofa. "I feel something. It makes my skin itch and makes my headache worse. I think the curse is there."

Saida cried out and stuffed her foot in my lap. My thigh burned where her sole laid on my jeans. I was fumbling to get the sandal off of her when Noah intercepted and did it for me. Nothing happened to my hand while my leg was still burning. "It's not the shoe."

I dropped it and picked up Saida's foot. I wasn't prepared and was immediately sucked into a memory of Saida sitting in a brown chair with her feet soaking in a tub of water at the base. The blue liquid bubbled around her calves. An attractive woman picked up one leg and ran a pumice stone over Saida's heel. She was giving Saida a pedicure. That was odd given what Lia has seen less than an hour ago.

I was in Saida's body which meant my muscles relaxed as the woman rubbed the bottom of her foot. She pushed her fingers into the arch next. A yelp left me, and I jerked my leg away just like Saida did in the memory. The sharp pain faded as fast as it happened. I was pulled out of the memory when Saida yanked her foot away. "What did you see?"

I gestured to her leg. "Look at the bottom. I think the lady that did your pedicure did something to you. The pain didn't come from tight tendons."

Saida's eyes clouded with worry as she did as I asked. The second she revealed the bottom of her foot, we could all see the rune that was glowing red on her skin. "We all got pedis together at Kassandra's place, Pretty Pebble Nails."

Lia's mouth gaped open as she stared at me. "I bet that's why I saw us getting pedicures."

I nodded in agreement. It was my first thought when I saw the memory. Fifi, Ella, and Natalie all sat on the floor and removed their shoes. A second later they stuck their feet in the air, revealing the same rune. I looked at Noah then back to Saida. "What does it mean?"

Saida's brow furrowed. "It's a syphon. They're taking our power, but why would Kassandra's employees do that? She doesn't need Fae magic."

"Who is Kassandra?" Lia asked.

Saida ran a hand through her hair. "Kassandra is the owner of Pretty Pebble. She's a gargoyle and isn't capable of using Fae magic. Not to mention, naturally she's a protector. All gargoyles are. I can't see her doing something like this. She loves us. We're her best customers."

"That's what we need to find out," Lucas replied. "I probably sound like a broken record, but the only person I know that needs energy right now is Laveau. I bet it was her and we need to find that out."

I cocked my head to the side. "Were the technicians new? Or were they the same ones that are usually there?"

Ella looked up from examining her foot. "They were totally new. I'd never seen them before. I asked Kassandra and she said her usual employees were injured."

Dahlia pursed her lips as she looked at the runes. "Can you remove the runes? We could try but we don't know enough about Fae markings and magic. I wouldn't want to hurt you."

Saida sucked her lips between her teeth then released them. "I'm not sure. This was made with a Dark object. I can feel the taint as I hover my finger over the top of it." She reached for Fifi's foot because she was closest to her and used her index finger to draw something on the sole of Fifi's foot. Saida grunted and did it several more times, then shook her head. "Nope. Nothing works."

Fifi squealed and kicked her leg. "Cut it out. I don't care what you have to do, but I want it off of me. I can't have a

Dark rune marking me. It will turn me." Fifi's hysterics didn't surprise me. I sensed she was highly emotional.

Saida grabbed her friend's foot and held onto it. "Calm down, Fifi. We need to think this through."

Ella wrapped her arms around her knees and laid her head in them. "There's nothing to think about. They did this believing we wouldn't resort to cutting ourselves. Nothing else will work. They want us weak and I'm not going to play their game."

I had to give the Fae women props. They considered carving out chunks of their flesh without flinching. The others nodded in agreement and Saida retrieved a small dagger from a bedroom. Because she owned a row house, I could see all the way to the back from where we sat in the living room.

Returning with towels, vodka, and water, Saida handed Lucas the dagger. Lucas jerked his chin at the alcohol. "Is that to clean the knife?"

Saida snorted. "Hell no. I need a couple of shots to get through this."

We all chuckled and then the Fae each took a big gulp of the vodka. Saida put her foot on Lucas's knee and Lia draped a towel underneath it. Saida closed her eyes and clenched every muscle in her body. She sucked in a breath and hissed as Lucas quickly sliced around the mark.

Delphine pulled a potion from her purse and pulled out the cork. "This will clean out any remaining taint that might be in the surrounding area." I sent Phi a grateful smile. As one of the nurses in the family, I typically did stuff like this, but I was too exhausted at the moment to do anything but watch.

Lucas moved Saida closer to Lia who wrapped her foot with gauze. Where the heck did she get that? It wasn't something we brought. Ella handed her some tape, answering my question. She must have grabbed the medical supplies.

Fifi screamed as if she was in full-blown labor when Lucas removed the symbol from her foot. Ella was silent and Natalie's reaction was somewhere between Fifi's shouting and Saida's grunting. The women were pale for several seconds while Phi and Lia cleaned them and the living room up.

Tears filled Saida's eyes as she looked at me. "What do we do about this? I can't believe Kassandra's employees did that to us. And I can't believe she would be involved."

My chest filled with warmth when I saw the Fae perk up and the circles under their eyes get lighter. "We need to pay Kassandra a visit and investigate whether or not she is involved." My sisters nodded in agreement.

Lia tilted her head from side to side. "Perhaps Albar will have some insight into Kassandra. Remembering the power of his stone form makes me shiver. It might be safer to go through Albar first, in case Kassandra has gone to the dark side."

Phi pursed her lips. "We can do that, but will it piss Kassandra off if we suggest she has done something wrong with her leader? It would make me mad if someone didn't talk to me first. I think we can get more information from her if we ask directly. They're known protectors. That means something. She wouldn't willingly do this which means we will be able to tell if she's lying."

I shrugged a shoulder. "That's a good point." I was still nervous about going but this wasn't something we could ignore. We'd been through a lot lately and I no longer shied away from the paranormal cases. Instead, I found myself wanting to know more as I sunk my teeth into the meat of the situation. It was like playing detective and we were getting good at it.

CHAPTER 17

DAHLIA

My eyes snagged on Lucas's fine ass as he moved through the kitchen. I'd been helping him prepare dinner, but exhaustion forced me to sit down. His daughter and her mate were coming for dinner at Willowberry. Lily had asked for the gathering and Lucas wanted her to get used to seeing him in this setting with me.

My nerves jumped as I prayed that she didn't blame me for taking him away from her and the pack. I knew all too well how stepchildren could be a pain in the ass, even ones that were fully grown. Dani's step-kids from her second marriage had been an adult-sized handful.

"Why aren't you up and cooking?" Dani asked as if my thoughts had conjured her. A knowing smile crossed her face. "Never mind, I can see you're enjoying the view."

I swatted my sister's arm. "Shut it. The truth is that I'm getting tired quicker. That potion Kip left me isn't working as long as it used to."

Concern creased Dani's face. "We need to get you to shift into a dragon, sestra. We can't have this hex weaken you. We aren't the Six Twisted Sisters without you."

I tried to smile and let her know I loved her too, but emotion choked me for several seconds. The truth was that none of us could survive without the others. We each played a different role with no one being more important than another. Kota had a knack for putting things together to make an event really shine. Design wasn't my strong suit.

Clearing my throat, I got up from the stool and crossed to get the salads from the fridge. We were having Cajun chicken and rice, with fruit and pasta salads. "I've been focusing on finding the heat in my core like we were told. I thought I found it this morning in the shower, but I got distracted." Heat crept over my cheeks as Lucas turned and leered at me.

Dani rolled her eyes. "I do not need to hear about that. After dinner we need to try again. With Lucas here, he can keep you grounded so that you don't freak out like I did." She held up her hand. "And, no there is need to worry about being able to shift back. Aside from Lucas, Dre and I are here. So are the pixies and there are a half a dozen shifters now living in the back cottages."

Noah and Lucas didn't like the idea of their mates being vulnerable and asked us if some of their people could live at Willowberry to keep an eye on us and help renovate the buildings. We had enough property that I didn't feel suffocated by their presence. Although, I did feel badly that they lived in less-than-ideal conditions. I couldn't imagine living in a building that was taken down to the studs. They were focusing on finishing one, so they had running water and electricity, but it was not done yet.

I handed the large bowl of fruit to Dani. "Take this out to the tables. Let me get through dinner first, then we can talk about me shifting. Or trying to, anyway."

Dani nodded her head and left with the fruit while I gathered plates and set the pasta on top of it. Lucas grabbed my arm before I left the kitchen. "There's no reason to be nervous. Lily loves you."

I went to my tiptoes and pressed a kiss to his lips. "You're right. Perhaps this curse is affecting me more than I realize." I found myself worrying about the wrinkles and saggy skin along the side of my jaw. Both of which had gotten much worse over the past week thanks to Marie Laveau. I hadn't let something so petty impact how I felt about myself for several years. However, these changes were drastic and had come on too fast to adjust to.

"All the more reason to try to shift tonight. And for the record, I would never have distracted you this morning if I'd known how close you were to finding the power of your dragon. In my defense, your fire drew me to you like a beast in heat."

That made my smile break out over my face. I'd loved how enthralled Lucas had been that morning when he joined me under the hot spray. He'd been in the kitchen making breakfast when he claimed to have smelled my need. He had given me several orgasms and helped me lock onto my heat in the process.

"I don't regret a thing," I promised him then patted his chest. "Finish plating the food up. Lily and Jeremy will be here soon."

I carried the plates and pasta salad outside and was surprised to see Kota and Dre along with their husbands, Steve and Jeff. They'd brought some homemade pizzas and a cooler full of drinks.

"What are you guys doing here?" I asked as I set my load down.

Kota popped a piece of pepperoni from one of the pies into her mouth. "We're here for moral support."

Dre nodded in agreement. "And it's a damn good thing too. We want to be here when you try to shift into your dragon."

I moved the pasta salad into the center of the table and spread the plates out. "You're always welcome when you come bearing pizza. Is that made with the dough from Nigel?" Nigel owned Hot Stone, the best pizzeria in town. It was more of an upscale Italian restaurant than your average pizza joint.

Kota sat forward with excitement. "Yep, it sure is. This dough is heavenly."

"It sure smells delicious." I startled and turned at the foreign voice. It was Lilyr. I knew her of course, but not well enough that I recognized her right away. "Thanks for having us over here. This place is special to us."

Her mate Jeremy smiled as he looked around. "It's nice to be back here but even better given that spread. I can never resist pizza."

"Does that mean you aren't going to eat my chicken and rice?" Lucas had an intimidating look on his face as he came out the door carrying a tray of the main course with Cami behind him carrying a covered dish. That must be the rice.

Jeremy ducked his head. "No, alpha. I love your food."

Lily smacked her father. "Stop intimidating my mate. We're here as family, dad. Not pack members."

Lucas beamed at his daughter and pressed a kiss to the top of her head. "You're right. But I wish I'd known you were making the pizza tonight, Kota. I'd have skipped all this work. I'd rather have what you made."

"It's not as if the food will go to waste. We can have leftovers for lunch or dinner tomorrow," Kota said as she served herself a slice and some fruit.

Jeff handed her a margarita in a can then got himself some chicken and a slice of pizza. "I'll take some to the girls, as well. They'll love this." I assumed Jeff was referring to their oldest daughter, Annabelle and her wife, Sarah. Not their two younger daughters. That's who they were usually talking about when they said the girls.

Laughter and conversation were easy as everyone filled their plates and started eating. It was Dani who broached the subject of why Lily had asked to have dinner with us. Dani was far more direct than I was. Dani was far more direct than I was. I preferred to allow people to tell me on their own time.

"So, why did you want to have dinner with your dad and Lia?" Dani asked around a mouthful.

Lucas drank the last of his beer, set the bottle down, then grabbed another slice of pizza. If the question bothered him, Lia couldn't tell. Lily grabbed Jeremy's hand and smiled at her father. "We wanted to tell you that you're going to be a grandfather."

Lucas's eyes went wide as he stared at his daughter for a second before he blinked and jumped to his feet. He picked Lily up and hugged her to him. "Congrats, sweetheart! I'm so happy for you both. When are you due?"

Jeremy brought Lily to his side when Lucas let her go. Lily placed her hand on her mate's stomach. "I'm due at the end of May."

Kota smiled at them. "Congrats. Looks like we will have to plan a baby shower for you guys."

I nodded in agreement. "I'm so happy for you both! It's such an exciting time. We will block off Willowberry any day you want for the shower. As soon as you know the theme for the nursery let me know and we can start the planning process."

Lily sat back down and took a sip of her soda. "We were thinking of rainbows, but we will have to wait to find out what we're having. Wynona said she can't tell for another six to eight weeks."

My forehead furrowed as I thought about how the pack healer would know the sex of the baby. "Does she have some special power to determine the sex of a fetus?"

Lily laughed. "Yeah, it's called an ultrasound machine."

I rolled my eyes and shook my head. "I should have known." I assumed everything in paranormal lives centered around magic.

Lily waved that comment away. "It's understandable."

Lucas was smiling as he cracked another beer. "How are you feeling? Any morning sickness?"

Lily frowned as she ran a hand over her stomach. "I have some nausea and cravings, otherwise it's just the need to pee all the time." That was thanks to the increased hormones at this stage of the pregnancy. Most people assumed that only happened in the last trimester. Lily sighed and her face smoothed as she smiled at her dad. "It's good to see you so happy dad. Perhaps we will have to add a mating ceremony to the shower."

Lucas frowned and turned his gaze my way. My heart skipped a beat. Here it was. I was just beginning to relax and let go of the worry that she was there to grill me about our relationship. "That's a day to celebrate you and your little one, not Lia and me."

Lily scowled at her dad. "You think I wouldn't be honored to share that day with you? Wait, you are getting mated, aren't you?"

My stomach squirmed and danced in response to her question. I wasn't ready to go there, yet. I liked how things were at the moment. God bless it, what did I say to her? Lucas saved me by pinning Lily with a serious expression that made my stomach churn. He didn't make us wait long for his response. "I appreciate you looking out for me, sweetheart, but it isn't necessary. Lia needs time before she's ready to take the next step and that's okay. When we do get mated things won't change from how they are now. I will still split my time between pack lands and Willowberry because Lia can't give up her life. She's too important to the future of the magical world here in New Orleans."

I laid my hand over Lily's. "I love your father and I'm not going anywhere. Except to try and shift into my dragon. I have got to shake Marie's hex." The urgency grew throughout dinner. I was going to wait so Lily, James, Jeff, and Steve didn't see me naked. I was going to shift and tear my clothes. I liked the shirt I was wearing but I wanted to fix this before permanent damage occurred. Lily's concern for her father's happiness made me realize how much was on the line if this curse progressed.

Lily's jaw dropped to her chest. "You're a dragon shifter? I thought you were witches. You have premonitions, right?"

I looked over at Dani then to Kota and Dre. "It seems we have several different genes within our cells. Dani is the only one that has managed a full shift, so far."

Kota held up a hand with talons instead of fingers. "But the rest of us can partially shift."

Jeff shook his head as he looked at Kota's hand. "I don't think I'll ever get used to this magic stuff."

Steve snorted and clapped Jeff on the back. "You should have been here during the zombie attack. Our wives were badasses. Yours made a machete appear out of thin air."

"And I saved your butt, too," Kota told Steve.

I pushed back from the table and stood up before this conversation went too far down that rabbit hole. Steve and Jeff had accepted our new lives with little issue. They'd been in the family long enough to know how to roll with the chaos. It just never used to be life or death matters like this.

"I'm ready to try and shift. Who's going to watch the

show?" I asked knowing everyone at the table would join us.

Cami lifted a blanket off the back of her chair. "I brought something to cover you after you turn back." I thought she'd brought it out because nights in November were chilly.

I smiled at the woman who had become an important part of our family. "Thanks, Cami. I was just about to run and grab something."

We all headed through the garden and to the back of the property where shifters were working on one of the buildings. Noah ran ahead of us and said something to the men. Before I knew it, they ran past us. I looked back and saw them descend on the food that we'd left out. My legs felt like they weighed a hundred pounds as we walked. I was tempted to ask Lucas to carry me. But I needed to do this on my own and use it as motivation to find my dragon. Something had to force that beast out.

"We won't have to worry about leftovers now. And, don't worry. I told them to leave enough for you to take to Annabelle and Sarah," Noah said from a few feet away.

Sweat poured down my back as we continued. Finally, we stopped in the middle of the yard. I squinted in the direction of the pixie mound. "Talewen!" I called out.

The tiny pixie flew from the small door built into the side of the hill. When they initially built their house, it was nothing more than a pile of dirt. Now it was shaped into a perfect dome and was covered in grass and colorful flowers.

Talewen and Jelin stopped in front of us. "What's up? Is something wrong?"

I shook my head from side to side. "Not at all. I wanted to warn you that I will be trying to shift into my dragon. I have no idea what will happen, so if there's a way for you to protect your home, please do it. I'd hate to stomp on it or burn it down."

Both pixies gasped and did this odd bounce while hovering. "Oh, exciting! Don't worry about us. We will all be watching and can rebuild easily." Talewen whistled and the rest of the pixies living in the mound came flying from their home.

I turned my focus inside to get this show on the road. It was difficult to concentrate on the heat in my core with so many eyes on me. I was painfully aware that everyone was watching and waiting to see if I would be able to do it. I forced those thoughts away again and again, but nothing happened.

Dani sidled up next to me and slipped her hand into mine. "Think about the heat you feel when you shifted your talons and follow that to its source. I'll do it with you."

I closed my eyes and focused on my talons before doing as Dani suggested. Intense heat radiated next to me sparking something in my chest. It was like a pilot light on a furnace had been lit and once it was burning bright, I was able to focus on it fully. When the temperature increased next to me, I fanned the flames inside me. I wasn't sure exactly what to do so I pictured what Dani's dragon had looked like with the wings and long snout.

My stomach churned and my muscles contracted within seconds. My mind seemed to go blank as something took over. I screamed when my bones broke and rearranged themselves before they grew. Agony was all I knew for several seconds as I felt my muscles and tendons join the Twister party.

My perception reeled as I grew taller. A screech left me as I realized the ripping sound was my clothing because I was actually shifting into a dragon. Before I knew it, I stood above everyone else except Dani. Recalling how Dani was enthralled by the gemstone, I kept my gaze focused on Lucas who stood several feet away. I looked from him to Dani who stood there in her dragon form like me.

I'd done it. Relief and joy made me giddy and I wanted to fly around the massive night sky. Flapping my wings, I lifted several feet off the ground. Something the size of my dragon's eye flitted in front of me and was waving her tiny arms. It took me a second to process that it was Talewen. "Your mate asked me to tell you not to take off into the night. He said he can't follow you."

He got his wish but not because I had listened to Talewen. I was still thinking about what she said when my back muscles ached as if I'd bench pressed hundreds of pounds and my wings stopped flapping. The disorientation of the shift and adjusting to the way my brain worked in this form was too foreign to control. Otherwise, I was certain I would have tried to go for a flight instead of stopping.

I fell with a hard thud to the earth sending dust up into the air. Now what? I had no idea how to shift back to my human form and I started to panic. My massive body flopped around on the ground, stopping Lucas from approaching me. It was the sight of three other dragons that stopped my worry from escalating. What the hell?

"It's your sisters," Lucas called out before he laid his hand on my hide. "It seems Kota and Dreya got caught up in the shift with the two of you."

"Holy fucking shit. My wife is a dragon! Steve, they're actually mythical creatures that could swallow us whole," Jeff muttered. He was standing behind Noah who was keeping he and Steve from approaching their wives.

A smile lifted my heart. We were stronger together. Suddenly knowing my sisters were in this with me made it much less scary and I was able to think about my human body. It seemed to take forever before my scales turned to flesh and my bones and muscles changed in reverse. I crawled to my sisters to join them under the blanket that Cami had thrown over them.

I looked at Kota and Dre "How the hell did that happen? Did you try to shift, too? Or did we pull you in?" When Dani and I combined our magic, it had been powerful enough to thwart Marie Laveau. It had to be capable of dragging Dre and Kota into the process, too.

Kota's gaze was focused elsewhere before she slipped out from under the blanket fully clothed. "I was thinking about the heat and my talons like Dani told you and, when I moved closer, I felt my magic click with yours. Before I knew it I was a dragon. And that process was fucking painful." Jeans and shirts appeared in her hand a second later and she gave them to the three of us.

Dre nodded as she pulled the shirt over her head. "The same thing happened to me. What a rush. I'd like to see that bitch try and take my sisters again. You will eat her for a snack."

I chuckled and ran my hands over my face after I got dressed. Lucas wrapped an arm around my shoulders. "You're beautiful, Flower. You have nothing to worry about."

Lily threw her arms around me. "You did great, Lia! You're something else. I'm so glad my dad found you. And just so you know how impressive that was, it took me three hours to shift back the first time I turned into my wolf."

James echoed a similar sentiment as I went back to checking on how I felt. Before shifting I had been so tired that I almost had to have Lucas carry me. No, I felt energized and better than I had before we were kidnapped. I was no healer, but I was certain that the hex Marie had placed on me was now gone. Relief made me giddy as I joined the conversation about how we could learn to control our dragon bodies. Steve and Jeff joined in with questions of their own. One problem was resolved. Now to find out if the Dark Fae and Marie were behind the runes placed on Saida and her friends.

CHAPTER 18

DANIELLE

Phi pursed her lips and crossed her arms over her chest as Lia drove to Pretty Pebble. "Why didn't you call Dea and I and let us know you were going to try shifting again last night? I would have come over so I could have tried, too."

Lia met Phi's blue eyes in the rearview mirror. "Because it wasn't planned. Lily came over to tell us she's expecting and then started grilling Lucas about when we were going to get mated. I'd been planning on trying again to burn away Marie's hex and used it as a way to escape the conversation. I didn't want Lily yelling at me for not wanting to get mated right now."

Delphine leaned forward, gripping the sides of the front seats. "Wow. I'll let you off for it this time. I can understand you not wanting to talk about that with Lucas's daughter. She's newly married and a young adult while you've lived a life most cannot even fathom. Just promise me that we will all try together. I'm curious what it's like. And I want to know how much power we can channel with the six of us connected. From what you guys describe, I bet it'll be epic."

Lia parked in a spot in front of the parlor and turned off the car. There was a huge picture window and a large woman standing inside the parlor talking to a Fae or an elf. I was surprised to see her brown hair pulled back into a ponytail, displaying her pointy ears.

Phi and Lia joined me on the sidewalk. "Remember to cast a locking spell to keep anyone from escaping if things go sideways. I don't want to run these bitches down." Lia and Phi nodded their agreement as we approached the door to the store.

The smell of nail polish and acetone assaulted my senses when I opened the door. The place was empty aside from the two women. It was like every other nail salon that I'd ever been inside. There was a row of chairs pushed against the large picture window behind us and in front there were six desks for manicures split into two with three on each side of the main aisle.

There were slim plastic shelves hung on one wall holding dozens of bottles of nail polish. There were chairs, with soaking tubs attached, arranged in a circle behind the desks. My toes tingled thinking about getting a pedicure. We might be there to find out who had marked Saida and her friends, but I was excited to get a pedi. It had been too long.

The large woman with curly brown hair turned and smiled at the three of us. "Welcome to Pretty Pebble. I'm Kassandra. Are you here for a mani, pedi, or both?" So, this was the gargoyle. She was exactly what I expected. She was taller than the average woman at six feet tall and her structure was larger, too. Her brightly colored moomoo concealed her muscular frame for the most part but I could see, based on her biceps, that she was strong.

Phi lifted her hands and smiled. "We're here for both. I called yesterday and made an appointment."

Kassandra glanced down at a paper calendar in front of her on the desk. "You must be Delphine, Dahlia and Danielle." Her head jerked up. "Are you one half of the famed Six Twisted Sisters?"

Phi inclined her head. "Yes, we are. How did you hear about us?" I was listening to the conversation but wondering why that got the other woman's attention. The employee's head jerked around and her eyes went wide for a second before she continued sorting through envelopes of sanitized instruments that had come out of an autoclave. Having worked in a hospital for decades, I was very familiar with those machines.

"Are you kidding? Everyone knows about the sisters that purchased Willowberry and put Marie Laveau in her place. Not to mention your fabulous parties. Word is that you throw the best parties," Kassandra explained.

It was interesting that the other woman glared at Kasandra when she mentioned us causing problems for Marie. She wore the scowl as she turned the water on in three of the soaking tubs. Kassandra stood up and motioned to the three chairs connected to the ones where the water was started.

Lia smiled and slipped out of her flip flops. "We haven't had an unhappy client, yet. Some of us, like Dani and Phi, have an uncanny ability to create the perfect design."

Kassandra smiled and called out to someone in the back of the salon. Another woman with dyed red hair joined them and pushed a small cart next to the water where Lia was soaking her feet.

The woman with the ponytail was helping me and it made me nervous to have her touch my feet. She poured crystals into my water while I wondered how to gather information. The best way was to tackle it head on. "So, how long have you worked here?"

The woman looked up at me with a sour expression. "What do you mean?"

Kassandra frowned at her employee. "Cilenne, don't be rude. She and Aryanna," Kassandra gestured to the other woman, "started here a couple of weeks ago when my regulars were injured."

That confirmed that these were the ones that we were looking for. "Have you done many Light Fae customers?" I asked as I watched the woman add more crystals to the water. Whatever it was made my skin tingle as it my feet were sitting in champagne. And it wasn't because of the jets. They hadn't been turned on yet.

Kassandra shifted her gaze from Phi's feet to my face. There was a knowing look in her eyes. "Why are you asking about my employees? Ask whatever you need to know plainly."

Lia and Phi joined hands and I reached out for Phi. I focused on locking the exits from the salon to keep the women trapped and muttered the spell to cast the enchantment.

Kassandra bolted to her feet making the ground shake. "What the hell are you doing? You didn't come here for a mani-pedi, did you?"

Lia held up her hands. "We would love nothing more than to come here and get our toes done. Fate, however, refuses to give us anything without a cost. We're here to find out why these women put Dark runes on the feet of countless Light Fae." Phi pulled the plastic bag from her purse and handed it to the gargoyle.

Kassandra looked at what we cut out of our friend's feet. Her skin rippled and turned gray for several seconds before returning to the light brown of moments ago. "What did you do? What is this? Who are you really?"

Cilenne glared at Kassandra then me. She said something under her breath and the water surrounding my feet began to boil. I tried jerking my feet out of the water but they wouldn't move. Kassandra shoved Cilenne out of the way and sliced a stone finger through the liquid. She hadn't shifted her entire form, only her hand. I scrambled from the seat and Phi and Lia did the same.

Cilenne shook her head. "We didn't do anything. I have no idea what this is."

Kassandra growled low in her throat. "Don't lie to me."

Aryanna spit at us. "You will regret getting in Marie's way. We did what we had to in order to heal her wounds. She'll be unstoppable when she brings Vodor back from the dead. Once he reclaims Eidothea, he will make sure Marie gets New Orleans.

Phi scoffed. "They survived Marie's kidnapping. She's not as powerful as you think. We are rooting out and destroying your work. How long before she's too weak to lift her head? Rest assured we will root out everyone helping her."

Kassandra's scowl was terrifying. "I can't believe you used my salon for ill intent. My clients rely on me to provide a safe service. I'm going to hand you both over to the council. They can decide how to punish you both. You both deserve to ponder your death as you sit in a cell in Coldwater Creek."

I looked at my sisters and jerked my chin at the Fae. We clasped hands and I did my best to form a clear image of freezing them both in place. *"Rigescunt indutae,"* we shouted together.

Cilenne screamed and jerked out of the spell we'd cast to hold her. It wasn't all that surprising that she was able to get out of it. We might be learning and getting more powerful, but we still had a long way to go. Kassandra went from a flesh and blood woman to a stone grotesquerie with wings and small horns on her head. She looked like a demon and sounded like rocks rubbing together as she bounded across her salon. Her stone hand wrapped around Cilenne's arm. A loud crack filled the room along with a pained cried from the Dark Elf. I had no doubt that Kassandra broke Cilenne's bone.

"Alright," Cilenne screamed. "Remzyn set up headquarters in a dwelling on Burgundy." Natalie scowled at her making Cilenne clamp her lips shut. Seemed like we weren't going to get much more out of her.

I liked seeing this vile woman get what she deserved. Cilenne took advantage of people that came to Pretty Pebble seeking some pampering. She did Marie's dirty work for her and planted a way for energy to be sucked from the innocent and given to Marie so she could live. That was as evil as Marie wanting to use me and my sisters to house her loa. I shook my head wondering how I'd gotten to the place that thinking about such violence didn't even faze me. I'd never been blood thirsty. And I wanted to help people, not hurt them. But I didn't flinch when I thought about Cilenne or Marie or any of the Dark Fae helping her being tortured or killed. I used to wish to have our simpler life back. Now, I only wished to maintain my caring nature. I didn't want it to become easy for me to hurt others, even in self-defense.

CHAPTER 19

DAHLIA

"Do you think those traitors lied to you guys?" Dea asked as we walked through the streets at the edge of the Quarter.

Cilenne had told us the street where the house was located thanks to Kassandra's inadvertent use of force with the Fae. The woman had answered with the threat of Kassandra looming over her and immediately regretted it. I tilted my head to the side and looked at Dea. "I think she was telling the truth. She was in too much pain to censor herself at first."

"I agree. What I worry about is whether or not the disappearance of the two women set off an alarm. We might find this place empty," Delphine added from behind us.

Dakota looked over her shoulder. "Let's hope not. I'd like to eliminate the Dark Fae that are a threat. Which makes me wonder if we're sure this potion works. We've used it three times now and have yet to see anything out of the ordinary."

I'd been wondering the same thing. Perhaps we'd done something wrong or had missed a step in the process. It was difficult to know for sure because we hadn't been able to test it.

Dre was walking next to Kota in front of Dea and I as she lifted one shoulder. "I trust Phoebe and because she talks highly of Fiona and her friends, I believe it works. We haven't come across them using a spell yet. It's possible they might not be using their magic to hide themselves here. After all, we have no way of determining if they're Light or Dark like Cyran does."

"What?" Cyran called out from the back of our group. He and Saida were bringing up the rear while Lucas and Noah were in the front.

The hair on the back of my neck stood on end. I sought out Lucas to see if he noticed anything. My heart started racing when I saw him stiffen then lift his hand into the air telling the rest of us to stop.

I patted the leather purse I wore across my shoulder. Kota had suggested we spend the day creating potions that would help us if we were overwhelmed. We had a potion that acted like acid, one that would incinerate a person, and others that did stuff like blind them.

We all crept forward as quietly as possible and crouched behind Lucas and Noah. The comfort from the body heat that I got from my sisters' proximity vanished when I caught sight of the beasts prowling around the yard of a house halfway down the block. They were the creatures we faced the first time we learned the Dark Fae were in town. The air shimmered slightly making me think the potion did indeed work. The pounding in my chest increased making me slightly dizzy. It could be the magic I felt building from the house behind the Fae monsters.

Phi tapped Lucas on the shoulder and pointed to herself

then the creatures between us and the front door. Lucas nodded his understanding then mouthed to Cyran that he would lead the charge through the door once the Fae were frozen by Phi and he and Noah would finish off the beasts before joining us inside.

My heart jumped into my throat when Delphine moved to the front of the group. I didn't like seeing her so exposed. If Phi was afraid, she didn't show it as she lifted her hands in the air and curved them in a half-circle. The beasts in the yard froze and Cyran ran past us. I wouldn't have known he had moved if I hadn't seen him. He was silent. My sisters and I sounded like a herd of buffalo in comparison.

I shivered as we hurried past the frozen monsters. Cyran didn't bother waiting as he broke down the door and moved into the house. I shared a look with Kota who was standing next to me. She dipped her chin down and gestured to the dark opening. From our vantage we couldn't see inside. We could hear shouting and flesh hitting flesh. It was the smell that frightened me and turned my stomach. It was coppery making me think of blood but it was mixed with an outhouse, rotten eggs, and hot trash. That was going to be hard to ignore.

Sucking in a breath, I walked through the door with my fingers shifted to talons. I considered conjuring my witch fire, but I couldn't risk burning down the house. We would be inside and there could be innocents in there. My breath caught in my throat when I caught sight of what was causing the stench.

What I could see of the floor through the mass of Dark Fae and mambos fighting Cyran and Saida was covered in blood. There was a pile of bodies in a corner. And Marie Laveau knelt next to an altar of sorts on the opposite side of the room. Her mambos were chanting and waving their arms. I needed to stop whatever they were doing, so I ducked around a guy with pointy ears and ran in their direction. I pulled a potion out of my bag at random and tossed it over my head aiming for the line of priestesses helping Marie with whatever ritual she was performing.

A Dark Fae woman lunged at me and caught me around the middle right after I let go of the vial. She took me down to the ground. Blood splashed up and hit my face. Bile rose to the back of my throat and a loud shriek echoed through the house at the same time. From the corner of my eye, I watched as one of the mambos swatted at one of her shoulders. I couldn't find out which potion I'd used because I had to move out of the way of the fist coming at me.

At the same time that I turned my head, I lifted my hands and sliced my talons through the woman's stomach. Rolling out from under her, I scanned the room. Dea was facing off with two Dark Fae males while Phi was fighting another and a mambo. Kota had a machete and was swinging it wildly while cursing up a storm. Dani was flinging potions at everyone she could. A hand fisted in my hair and yanked me off of the ground. Reaching up, I cut as much of the arm holding me as possible.

"Bitch," a deep voice snarled in my ear. Something cold and sharp pierced my side. I cried out and pressed a hand to the wound as blood dripped out and splashed on the already saturated floors. "Your powers will be added to the collective."

With a snarl, I twisted my body around. It wrenched my hair painfully, but I didn't care. One of my talons cut through the guy's forearm making his fingers go limp. It was easy to hit the right place now that I was facing him. To my horror the guy snarled and shifted his appearance becoming a wolfman hybrid creature. It was nearly identical to the skin walker I'd seen in my very first vision.

"Not this time, asshole," Xinar declared. I hadn't seen him

join us, but he was suddenly there and grabbing hold of the skin walker. The skin walker hissed at the UIS agent and took off running. I lost track of them both as they moved through the melee. There were too many in the room fighting. I pulled another vial from the bag and slammed it into the chest of a Fae coming after me. She screamed as her shirt melted followed by the skin covering her chest.

Not wanting to see the rest, I pulled out another vial and noticed several men and women frozen throughout the room. That had to be Phi's doing. Lucas and Noah joined the fight as I hurried to the closest immobile person and splashed the potion on him. I had three more bottles and decided to use them on the ones Phi had frozen. I managed to hit one more with the spelled liquid. However, the second vial slipped from my hand when the guy suddenly regained his ability to move and wrapped a hand around my neck.

The oxygen was cut off and my vision started to go gray at the edges. I thought I saw Remzyn swing a broad sword and slice through Noah's right arm at the shoulder. I panicked when I witnessed my sister's mate get injured. Dani couldn't lose Noah. She, more than most, I knew deserved the love and happiness she'd discovered with Noah. I growled and regained my ability to think, dropped the potion and raked my hands down the Fae's face that was holding me. He dropped me so suddenly that I wobbled and had to catch myself on the wall.

Remzyn shouted something in a foreign language then took off through the back of the house. Several other Dark Fae broke away from the fighting and went to Marie Laveau who shot me a victorious smile. Dani partially shifted into her dragon and used her wings to batter those around her. I was very aware of the massive dragon prowling around. Her wings touched the sides of the walls. Kota continued cutting down Fae and mambos while Dre took out the ones that Phi kept freezing. Marie was losing. Why was she smiling? I glared at the Queen of Voodoo who flinched before she allowed a group to usher her to the back of the house.

I took off to follow and slipped in a puddle of blood. My skull bounced off of the hardwood floor painfully. Lucas pulled me up before my head could hit it again. "They're already gone. The rest took off."

Why the hell would they do that? They had us outnumbered. Although, we'd done a good job of cutting their numbers. I'd say that Marie was still weak and didn't want to chance facing Lucas again, but that didn't seem right.

Bracing myself on my knees, I scanned the blood-soaked room and it hit me. We had walked into a trap. Marie got what she needed from us and left. I had no idea what that was because all of us had survived. It was highly satisfying that I couldn't say the same for Marie's mambos and the Dark Fae. Some had escaped, but their group had also lost several people.

Dea shook her head next to the door. "We're screwed, sestras."

Dre wiped her forehead with the back of her hand and winced. She'd taken a board to the right cheek during the fight. "What do you mean? And how was this bitch able to fight us without the magic of the council biting her in the ass?"

Dea sighed and turned away from the window. "We might have dealt a blow to the Fae causing problems in the French Quarter. However, one of them is now playing host to Baron Samedi. The loa rose from the blood and bonded with a dark-haired Fae. He's now corporeal and I have no idea what that will mean for us or the city." Holy shit. Marie used the many deaths and blood to raise the loa.

Anger surged through me. "We played right into that vile woman's plans. God bless it, I wish you had ripped off her head last time we fought her, Chief. Now she's working with the skin walker and the Dark Fae. *And* she managed to bring one of her loa to life. A god with immeasurable power is a whole new level of danger." I leaned my head against Lucas's shoulder as he stood close to me.

Dani shook her head as she held Noah to her side. His head was sagging and his side was bleeding. "We can't change what's already happened. We will find a way to separate Samedi from the Fae no matter how hard it is. And, we have the council to help. None of us know how Marie was able to violate the terms of the contract. But I have to believe that there will be magical repercussions for her. There'd be no other reason to have us all sign the agreement."

Noah was clutching his right arm, covered in sweat, and pale. That guy was seriously powerful to survive an injury like that and still be standing. "The only explanation I can come up with is that the magic hasn't reacted to the violation yet. Kaitlyn used powerful spells to ensure that no one used enchantments to fool the binding agreement. We will need to ask Kaitlyn if she can find out what happened."

Dani sighed as she clutched Noah tighter. "That can be looked into later. Right now, we have some wounds to heal and a party to throw."

I smiled at Dani. Obsessing on the danger we now faced wouldn't help any. Dani was right. We'd already faced a lot of crap and survived. The six of us were strong together and we would tackle Samedi and Marie in due time. Being part of a momentous event like this anniversary party was the perfect reminder about why helping stop Marie and her evil loa was so important.

CHAPTER 20

DANIELLE

Cami rushed past me carrying two flower arrangements for the gift table we set up near the edge of the covered patio, between the main house and the catering kitchen. It was where we set up the food and tables for most parties. We had ceiling fans and heaters for the winter months. The hanging twinkle lights and café lights made the area glow with soft yellow light.

Brezok had the bar set up. The wine glasses Lia had made for the anniversary party made a beautiful display with their interlacing rings that said *fifty years of mated bliss*. Lincoln's glass said *I still do what she says,* while Gracie's said *I still do* with a ring for the 'O' on both. The caterer was busy moving the food from the kitchen to the warmers on the table while the DJ was testing his system.

Dre turned me, putting her hands on my shoulders. "You should go sit with Noah. Everything is ready. Dea is making sure the balloon arch is attached securely to the wooden backdrop since it's windy. There's nothing left for you to do."

I sighed and glanced around, my gaze stopping on Noah who was sitting at a table off to one side out of the way. "Thanks, Dre. It turned out great. I love the picture frame around the wolves. It was a great addition." Dre had suggested that we have Lia's oldest daughter paint images we had cut out, of two wolves standing together, to match what Gracie and Lincoln's wolves looked like. The wood cutouts were wearing a wedding dress and a tux. Initially, I wasn't so sure. Now, I loved the sign because it was so realistic. We had engraved the dates in the middle of the ornate frame.

I took the chair next to Noah and scooted closer to him. "How are you feeling? You didn't overdo it, did you?" Noah's arm had almost been cut off by the Dark Fae leader, Remzyn.

Noah leaned over and pressed his lips to mine. "I've never been better. Gracie and Lincoln are going to love this surprise."

"I hope so. I'd love it if one of my kids arranged a surprise like this for me." I couldn't sit with Noah as the guests started arriving. I got up and helped lead them to a table after Lucas greeted them. The party was a surprise, so everyone was arriving before the couple.

Lia came running from the parking lot. "They're coming. Cut out the lights."

A smile crossed my face as I flicked the switch plunging the area into semi-darkness. It wasn't completely black, thanks to the moon in the sky and the lights in the main house.

I smelled Noah's cologne before he wrapped an arm around my waist where I was waiting to turn on the lights when the couple and their daughter arrived. "I love you, Sunshine." Noah's hot breath tickled my ear.

"I love you, too," I whispered.

Footsteps echoing on the sidewalk were accompanied by a woman asking what they were doing at the plantation. Stasia didn't get a chance to respond before her father followed her mother's question with one of his own. "Did the alpha summon us? Is he calling me into service to protect the pack?"

Stasia sighed and I saw her shake her head. "No dad. That's not what's happening." Stasia lifted her left hand and held up a finger signaling me to turn on the lights. I flicked the switch and the crowd yelled, "Surprise!"

Gracie gasped and tears filled her eyes when her gaze landed on the happy fiftieth banner that we'd made from laser cut pieces. That was Phi's project for the event. It was the biggest one she'd done yet. It stretched from the house to the catering kitchen. The colors of the letters and triangular pieces alternated between gold, cream and black to match the rest of the decorations.

The couple hugged their daughter before moving through their friends, laughing and talking. After Noah congratulated them, he moved me to the bar and ordered me a swamp water. I hadn't gotten anything the other night when I'd gone to dinner with my sisters. We took our drinks to the table in the corner and were joined by the others. Typically, we would mingle throughout the party making sure the guests had everything they needed. Lucas had insisted we allow his shifters to do that for us. It suited me just fine. I was all-in when we planned the party and got ready for it. But, when it actually started, I wanted to disappear. I didn't want to be part of it. For me the event was about making something that brought happiness and improved life just a little.

"This turned out fantastic," Dea said as she sipped her cocktail. "Can you imagine what we could have done for mom and dad on their fiftieth if we'd had this place, or Lacie?"

Lia smiled as her gaze went distant. "We did good with what we had back then, but we would have rocked their sixtieth if they'd made it that far."

Dre's eyebrows furrowed and she got to her feet. "What are they doing here?"

I followed her gaze, and my heart skipped several beats. Cyran, Alar, and Kaveh were placing gifts on the table along with Kaitlyn. Why the hell were members of the Aegis council at this party?

Lucas waved at the newcomers. Kaveh acknowledged us as he diverted his steps to congratulate the couple that was drinking and talking with their friends on the dance floor. Music was playing but no one was dancing yet. We had set up the corn hole games and the large Jenga along with lawn darts and several people were engaged in those activities. It was a relief to see that no one reacted to the arrival of these leaders.

"Stasia invited them when she heard about the council because Gracie and Lincoln know them. She's embracing the changes like most in the pack," Lucas explained.

Cyran and Kaitlyn followed Kaveh's lead and congratulated the couple while Alar joined our table. He scowled when he glanced over and noticed what the others had done. "Excuse me," Cyran told us before he crossed to the couple.

"I'm going to grab some beers and a pitcher of pina coladas," Steve said as he stood up.

Lucas clapped him on the back. "Thanks, man. I was just going to do that while they greeted the guests of honor."

Steve returned as the DJ announced the food was ready. The guests rushed the long line of food, set out like a buffet. Gracie and Lincoln were at the front with Stasia who was smiling from ear to ear. The council members joined us at our table.

Kaveh sat down next to Kaitlyn who shifted uncomfortably when the djinn kissed the back of her hand. Cyran snorted and shook his head. "You've been back in the city for less than a month and you're already romancing the ladies. Leave some for the rest of us."

Kaveh rolled his eyes. "The djinn haven't been living under a rock, you know. We aren't going to come in here and steal all the available women. And, I'm sure Kaitlyn resents being talked about as if she doesn't have a say in her love life."

Kaitlyn sighed in exasperation. "My love life is not up for discussion. But to set the record straight, I am the only one that makes decisions about who I get into a relationship with."

Cyran chuckled as he accepted a beer from Steve. "I like a feisty woman. I meant no offense, Kaitlyn. I was teasing Kaveh. You can loosen up, buddy. Life shouldn't give you an ulcer."

Kaveh chose to ignore Cyran altogether as he turned to me. "I received some fantastic news and would like to hire the Six Twisted Sisters to host an event for my kind."

Delphine jumped up and ran inside the house. I was certain she was getting her iPad since she was the one that kept us organized. I inclined my head and took a sip of my drink. "We would love to help. What kind of an event do you want to throw? A welcome back to New Orleans?"

Kaveh looked at me as he peeled the label from his bottle of beer. He seemed lost in thought and didn't appear to be aware of what he was doing. "I'd like to amend that. It seems I have two events I'd like to have you host. A get to know you party for the djinn that decide to return to this city is a perfect idea. Many of my kind are withdrawn and wary. But

I was asking about a baby shower. I discovered my best friend's sister is pregnant. She's the first pregnancy we've had in five years."

Lia gasped and her hand went to her chest. "I had no idea that djinn fertility was so low. I can see why you'd want to celebrate it. Is that normal for your kind?"

Phi returned to the table. "What'd I miss?"

Kota gestured to Kaveh. "We're going to host two parties for the djinn. One is a mixer for those moving back to New Orleans and the other a baby shower. They don't have babies often, so this is a big deal."

"That sounds very exciting. We haven't done a baby shower here at Willowberry yet. When did you want to have these parties? And what themes are you thinking about?" Phi asked as she opened our calendar.

Kaveh turned to Kaitlyn with a panicked expression on his face. "I'd like the return party soon. The baby shower will be in a few months. Themes? I wouldn't know where to begin. I trust you not to steer me wrong. Can you help me with these?"

I shot Lia an amused expression. Kaveh was hiring us for our expertise in planning and preparing events, yet he was asking the woman he had barely stopped staring at since he arrived. I had to give it to him. It was a great way to get Kaitlyn to spend some time with him.

Kaitlyn sucked in a breath then started coughing. Some of her pina colada must have gone down the wrong pipe. "Me? Why would you ask me? They are far better suited to help with this kind of stuff."

I smirked at Kaitlyn. "But he trusts you, Kaitlyn. We're happy to help with ideas, of course. As an aside, can you tell us what happened to Marie and Remzyn for going against the council agreement? I've been curious for the last two days and can't stand it anymore."

Kaitlyn glanced around to see who was close then cast a sound barrier so no one could hear what we discussed while leaving us able to hear what was going on around us. "The punishment for breaking a magical contract is typically swift and severe. Marie and Remzyn were careful to use their kind as sacrifices to complete the ritual to give Samedi a corporeal body. Remzyn had far more leeway and used the Dark Fae because I had only previously designated the Light Fae. It was an oversight. I've since corrected that. The reason they retreated so fast was because they lost their power the second Remzyn attacked Noah. What you didn't see was the crippling pain they endured, as well. At least that's what should have happened. Unfortunately, Marie had already completed her goal when that occurred. It was Lia's blood that allowed the loa through."

"Does that mean they no longer have their power?" Dre asked.

Cyran set his empty beer bottle on the table. "Don't be daft. They got their powers back the second they met up with her god."

What use was having this agreement if we couldn't enforce it? "This council is pointless. They'll continue attacking us."

Kaveh held up a hand. "This agreement might seem largely symbolic, but it carries significant weight. It has been boosted by a donation of magic from every faction but theirs. There have always been disagreements and fights. The magical world is violent. However, people have already reported fewer incidents. And it does give us something we can use to slow offenders. Ideally, she would be captured and imprisoned for her actions. Marie gets her power from fear like yours. If you believe she is an all-powerful god she becomes one."

The tinkling of metal on glass interrupted our conversation. Kaitlyn removed the silencing spell that was around us while we looked at Gracie and Lincoln who were standing with Stasia. Gracie lifted a hand. "We wanted to take a moment to thank our wonderful daughter for throwing us the best surprise party in the world. Everything about tonight is perfect. I don't know where you got the pictures of us for this. I haven't seen some of them in decades. We'd also like to thank the Six Twisted Sisters for all of their hard work. You've made our night extra special. We especially love how you managed to make our wolves look elegant and graceful. Your creativity is astounding."

Lincoln cleared his throat. "I'd like to echo what my Gracie said. We love you, Stasia. We couldn't have asked for a better daughter. And I'd like to add that the changes to the magical community have been sorely needed. I'm still astonished that six mundies that haven't had their magic for very long have managed to turn everything on its head. I never thought I would see my good friend, Kaveh, within these city limits again. To Stasia and the Six Twisted Sisters."

Everyone cheered and clinked glasses. I touched mine to Noah's then all of my sisters. That was a heavy toast. And it made me proud to be part of this group. We were amateur detectives at best, but what we lacked in experience we made up for in raw determination. It was amazing what you could do when six great minds got together.

As the guests resumed their eating, dancing and drinking, I decided to get some food. The swamp water was going to my head. Or maybe it was the joy of the moment. It was doing these events that made it possible for me to say I would be ready for the next paranormal crisis when it happened. And God knows there would be plenty more of them to come. I shoved aside thoughts about Samedi, and the Fae he inhabited, along with how we could stop Marie from breaking the rules that she'd agreed to. Those were worries for another day. Right now, I was feeding my body and soul.

Download the next book in the Twisted Sisters' Midlife Maelstrom series, Etou-Fae the Hard Way HERE! Then turn the page for a preview.

EXCERPT FROM ETOU-FAE THE HARD WAY BOOK #5

DAHLIA

"We need to get the stuff to make the *bahn mi* sandwiches," Kota said as she turned the corner pushing the cart. We were in one of the bulk stores buying food and necessities for the week. It had been a quiet couple of days since Marie managed to stuff Baron Samedi in a body, so we were taking the opportunity to grab what we needed while we had the chance.

My mouth watered when she mentioned the sandwich that she'd created based on our favorite Vietnamese restaurant. "We need the pork tenderloin and buns. We still have the radish, carrots, and cucumber for the slaw."

Kota scanned the freezers as we walked down the aisle, stopping at the fish section. "I wish we could find the crusty rolls they use at the restaurant. Those would make them even better."

I lifted a shoulder as I grabbed some shrimp, orange roughy, and tortilla crusted tilapia. "We should ask Lucas and

Noah if they know any place that might have them. They seem to have a vast knowledge about food in this city."

Kota snorted and waved a hand down the front of her body. "You'd think it would be me with that knowledge."

Setting the frozen fish in the basket, I frowned at my sister. "Why? You never eat out. And don't say because of your weight. You're beautiful and, with all these cases, you're moving more and improving your health. That's what matters. Now, is there anything we need to get for the tea party?"

Dakota continued walking with a smile on her face. Getting magic had helped us all in different ways, but it was good to see Kota confident despite the extra weight she carried. "Who throws a tea party for a bachelorette party, anyway? I've never heard of such a thing. Although, I have to admit, I can't wait to see the low tables Dani and Dre are making. The big teal cushions I ordered for them to sit on will be perfect for the outdoor setting."

My thoughts echoed Kota's. It made me feel old to think that wasn't how it was done when I was younger. When I was in my twenties women would go on short trips or do the traditional party of naughty clothing, drinking, and strippers. One more reminder I was in the middle of my life. My age wasn't something I thought about that often.

Back to the tea party, Kota and Dani had come up with an exquisite boho-chic theme for the event next week. "It's better than getting drunk and not remembering your night."

Kota chuckled and grabbed a bag of tortilla chips. "I can't imagine going out and drinking like we used to twenty years ago. I'd rather be at home of Willowberry. We should grab some of those nice plastic plates. I don't want these women breaking the China in our grass. And Fred would be pissed if his lawn mower breaks because we missed a shard."

That was a brilliant idea. It would save having to clean

dishes afterward, as well. "Thats not a bad idea. How many are coming again?" There was a woman ahead giving out samples of a pot sticker. My stomach rumbled, reminding me that I hadn't eaten breakfast. We would have to try what she had to offer.

Kota scanned the freezer to our left as we walked. "Heidi said at least seventy-five. That's another thing. Who has that many friends? I had ten at mine and half of them were my sisters. How can it be personal with so many there?"

We were accustomed to large parties in our family. Just getting the ten siblings together with their families was over sixty people. I used to be embarrassed by how big my family was. Now I was happy to share about them with anyone that would listen. And, I couldn't imagine not having them. "That would be our immediate family along with Aunt Shelly's family. However, I get the feeling from Heidi that this doesn't involve any family. It seems that they come from money. I got the impression that this is more about making a show than anything else. Heidi wanted to do something unique for her friends."

Kota snorted. "High tea at a plantation with custom platforms and boho-chic décor is definitely that."

My chuckle died off as the smell of soy sauce, sriracha, and garlic combined with grilled vegetables permeated my nose. I had one of my legs lifted to take the next step when dizziness sent me stumbling into Kota.

My vision swam and the smell of Chinese food cooking in a skillet was all I could focus on. The scent was overwhelming, making me think that I was standing in the middle of a bustling restaurant kitchen. I'd waited too long to eat after running six miles this morning. I couldn't keep doing that for fear we would be attacked at any minute.

Or the big ass fans on the ceiling of the warehouse store

were blowing the scent in our direction. My heart skipped a beat as another thought struck me. I shook my head trying to clear it. None of that was right. There was something magical happening to me at the worst possible moment. Kota reacted quickly and wrapped an arm around my waist.

Before my mind fully comprehended what was happening, my vision wavered and the store disappeared. My heart raced and my mind whirled as I tried to understand what I was seeing. I was standing in the living room of a friend from high school.

I hadn't seen Amy or her kids for at least a year, but I would recognize her smile anywhere, even if her hair was now dark brown with teal, purple and pink streaks like a unicorn. I wished what I was seeing was as cute and friendly as the mythical creatures. It wasn't.

There was a light-haired woman dressed in the maroon robes of Marie Laveau's mambos standing over Amy, who was bleeding from several wounds and tied to a chair. The mambo looked familiar, but I couldn't place where I'd seen her. Was she one of the ones there the other night when Marie brought Baron Samedi, the voodoo loa of resurrection. Also, he is often called upon for healing by those near or approaching death. I have no doubt he had helped Marie heal the rest of the way from the injury Lucas had inflicted. More of the voodoo lore surrounding him was that it was only the Baron that could accept an individual into the realm of the dead, so what happened now when one of his followers died?

Giving myself a mental head shake, I focused on what I was seeing. I was being given this vision for a reason. There was a wok on the stove behind Amy that was sizzling making me wonder if she was cooking something.

I turned my head and noticed another person sitting

across from Amy in a wingback chair that he'd pulled over from the living room. He looked like a Dark Fae I'd encountered before. I recognized his piercing violet eyes. He smiled at Amy and clasped his hands together, laying them on his stomach. "Give us the information we want and this will all end. I'll even be sure to erase your memory so you aren't haunted by our little visit." The mambo was leaning on the counter listening to the exchange.

Amy glared daggers at the guy and clenched her mouth shut. Good girl. It was obvious that was a lie. Why had they gone to her house? There was no obvious connection between me and her. I wracked my brain for how they could have found her as I watched the mambo pick up a metal stick with something at the end. It looked like a symbol but I didn't recognize it. She chanted something in Creole before she pressed the now glowing metal to Amy's upper chest. Her shirt had been burned in so many places that the fabric hung from her shoulder nearly exposing her breast.

My stomach roiled as they continued to inflict pain on her. The Dark Fae and mambo kept demanding that Amy give them the information they'd asked for without repeating it. Since I was the one that was friends with her, it had to be related to me. Were they punishing her for us creating the Aegis council? I was certain that Marie lost her powers after she betrayed the agreement the head of every species had signed in blood. That had to have pissed her off.

Again, how did they find Amy? The only explanation I could come up with was that I listed my high school on my Facebook page. They could have looked for a yearbook from when I graduated. In it they'd find plenty of pictures of Amy with me and Kristen. My heart stopped and I screamed when I saw the guy leap from his seat with a snarl and slash a dagger across Amy's throat. I swear the Dark Fae looked in my direction when I shouted.

The world swam around me again and the fluorescent lights of the warehouse store blinded me as I came back to Kota. She was running her hand up and down my back while cooing at me. I cringed when I saw that there were a number of people surrounding us.

"Her husband was killed, and the grief hits her at odd moments," Kota explained to the group. None of what she said had been a lie. I was haunted by Leo's death at times and it would hit me out of the blue. The same with my mother's death. There was no such thing as closure. You learned to live with part of your heart missing, but it never grew back. It was easier now that I had Lucas and it rarely affected me anymore. Yet, my love for him couldn't erase my past or what had happened to Leo.

"I'm better now. Thanks. Sestra." I grabbed her hand and pulled her along, pushing past the gaping crowd.

I didn't say anything until we reached the meat section. It was relatively empty because the customers had all flocked to the frozen foods aisle to see what was going on with me. Talk about bad timing for visions.

Kota grabbed the pork tenderloin. "What the hell did you see? You were out for nearly a full minute."

My shoulders shook with repressed tears. "They killed Amy."

Kota stopped next to the bread and turned to face me. "What?" In hushed whispers, I told her what I had seen as we gathered the rest of the groceries we needed. "We need to head home, grab the others, and get to Amy's house."

I sniffed as I nodded in agreement. I was grateful that I didn't even have to suggest it. None of my sisters would leave a friend to be hurt like that. We paid the bill and I drove way too fast from the store to the plantation. Kota called and told them what had happened so Dre, Cami, Dea, and Dani were waiting when we arrived.

Dre gestured to her car. "Cami will unload the groceries. We're going to Amy's house."

I nodded and climbed out from behind the wheel. I shouldn't have driven home. I didn't recall any of the trip. All I could think about was I had time. All of my visions came before an event happened.

Dre drove ten miles over the speed limit only slowing when we hit school zones and a little over ninety minutes later, we pulled up to the curb in front of Amy's house. A loud noise from inside practically made me jump out of my skin. I ran up the sidewalk and knocked on the door. I will never forget the muffled scream from inside.

I twisted the knob and stopped breathing. The Dark Fae stood there glaring at me with the knife dripping blood in his hand. How the hell was this possible? I should have had days. I always had ample time to fix the problem before it actually happened. Without thinking, I launched myself through the door and right at the asshole. Dani and Kota hurried to Amy's side while Dea and Dre faced off with the mambo.

Luckily, we caught them off guard. They clearly weren't prepared to face us as their first instinct was to turn toward the back door but not before they tossed spells at us. I felt the energy leave the Fae and curled into a ball mid-motion. It made me drop to the ground with a thud. I was too numb to feel anything. The crackle of a hex sizzled above me and headed for Dre and Dea. Kota shouted and lifted a massive silver shield into the air before the enchantment hit them. The metal sent the curse spinning back on its caster. The mambo and Dark Fae cursed then took off running.

Uncurling, I stood up and clenched my hands into fists. "Holy shit, we were too late. How did this happen? I usually have more time." A vice closed around my heart. Amy didn't deserve to be dragged into this mess.

FRENCH QUARTER FAE

Dre's hand ran up and down my back as she stood next to me. "I can see you blaming yourself. You can't do that."

"I have to be the reason they were here. Amy isn't paranormal. There's no reason for them to hurt her like that. God, what do we do?" No one said a thing as we stood there looking at Amy. Finally, I had to avert my eyes. My mind refused to work through the problem and come up with a solution. The images from my vision kept replaying in my mind, making the ache in my chest worse.

Dani's phone rang, breaking the silence in the house. My stomach was in knots. I was too late to save one of my closest friends growing up. Why had they killed her? Amy had nothing to do with the magical world. Rage, grief, and determination battled it out for supremacy in my mind. I wanted to find those assholes and make them pay for hurting my friend. They would not get away with this. Lucas and his shifters would help in the hunt. Surely with that much manpower behind the task I would find the people that did this and make sure they suffered for an eternity.

I was distracted from the roiling of my emotions by Dani's wide eyes and loud gasp. I shifted so I stood next to her. "Wait, I'm going to put you on speaker so you can repeat that." Dani hit a button and held the phone aloft between us. Dre, Dea, and Kota moved closer to Dani so they could hear. Their proximity helped me hold myself together.

"I had a premonition during my afternoon lecture. It was scary as hell and I almost didn't make it out of the classroom," Phi said into the speaker on her side. "The amulet works like a charm to warn me that something is coming. I've been practicing by trying to force a prophecy so I can increase the time I have. I thought it was pointless until today. I managed to make it down the hall to my office and slam the door shut."

Kota scowled as we listened. "Shit. I'm sure it was probably useful. You've never gotten one that didn't mean something, but you can't remember anything you are given."

Phi's sniff was louder that it should be coming through the speaker. It sounded as if she was in the room with us. I could even picture her chin lifting into the air as a smirk crossed her face. "I hit the record button on my phone immediately so I would know what I said."

I couldn't help my chuckle of appreciation hearing what Phi just said. She was freaking brilliant. "That was smart thinking, sestra. Play it for us."

"I'll try. I might need to call you back from my office phone if the app won't do it while I'm talking to you," Phi said as the sound of movement joined her words. There were a couple of seconds of that before Phi got back on the phone. "I'll call you right back."

The phone went dead and I stared at Dani. "That could have been a disaster if she hadn't escaped to her office. She's got to be pissed it interrupted her class. She just got back to a hundred percent after the cancer and now this. I feel awful for her."

Dani nodded her head. "Phi is excited about having another power. And she's going to be the best seer the magical world has ever seen. She doesn't do anything half-assed."

Dani was right. Delphine put all of her effort into every event that we did. And she was always a part of the entire process. She was the only one of us, aside from Dani, that was capable of doing everything from coming up with ideas to planning them to executing them. The rest of us participated and threw out suggestions, but we had strengths in specific areas. If you could call being a worker bee a strength because that's where I excelled. That and running the laser.

Phi called back and Dani put her on speaker. "Alright, sestra. Let's hear it."

The cold, deep voice Phi adopted when she was lost in a trance echoed through the tiny speaker. It made her sound even more otherworldly than usual during one of her visions. *"The collision of worlds exposes the Twisted Sisters' weaknesses. All is in peril if action isn't taken. Only removing the spokes of the wheel will offer a solution."*

My heart raced in my chest as a chill raced up my spine. Standing in the living room of Amy's house, with her dead a few feet away, was not the best time and place to hear something so cryptic and haunting. "What does that even mean?"

"You know I don't get instructions with these things. I'm lucky recording it allowed me to hear what I said. I don't even sound like myself," Phi replied.

Dani shook her head from side to side. "You sound like you're possessed by another entity entirely. If I didn't know you were still yourself after this, I would worry that somehow Marie put one of her loa into you."

Phi's breath caught. "I don't like what we are facing one bit."

Amy's lifeless form haunted me from the corner of my eye. "Tell me about it. We're standing in Amy's house. She was killed by two of the people working with Marie Laveau and Remzyn."

Phi's sharp intake of breath almost shattered my resolve. I'd managed to hold back the tears and grief so far. I didn't want to lose my shit now. We had to make sure her kids didn't come home and find their mom like this, and to make sure there was no hint of the paranormal left behind.

Anger tried to steal my reason. I couldn't grieve for my friend because I had to worry about keeping the existence of paranormals hidden. I should be able to cry and yell and scream at anyone I needed about the injustice of Amy's death. She was a kind person that deserved so much more than she got. I'd make sure her kids were always looked after. After all, her death was my fault.

You can't blame yourself, Lia. You don't control what evil does. Logically, I knew that was true, but it didn't matter when I was faced with the reality of what had happened. Logic went out the window when your heart got involved whether it was from love, grief, or anger. Strong emotions tended to take over and obliterate all else.

AUTHOR'S NOTE

Reviews are like hugs. Sometimes awkward. Always welcome! It would mean the world to me if you can take five minutes and let others know how much you enjoyed my work.

Don't forget to visit my website: www.brendatrim.com and sign up for my newsletter, which is jam-packed with exciting news and monthly giveaways. Also, be sure to visit and like my Facebook page https://www.facebook.com/AuthorBrendaTrim to see my daily posts.

Never allow waiting to become a habit. Live your dreams and take risks. Life is happening now.

DREAM BIG!

XOXO,

Brenda

OTHER WORKS BY BRENDA TRIM

The Dark Warrior Alliance
Dream Warrior (Dark Warrior Alliance, Book 1)
Mystik Warrior (Dark Warrior Alliance, Book 2)
Pema's Storm (Dark Warrior Alliance, Book 3)
Isis' Betrayal (Dark Warrior Alliance, Book 4)
Deviant Warrior (Dark Warrior Alliance, Book 5)
Suvi's Revenge (Dark Warrior Alliance, Book 6)
Mistletoe & Mayhem (Dark Warrior Alliance, Novella)
Scarred Warrior (Dark Warrior Alliance, Book 7)
Heat in the Bayou (Dark Warrior Alliance, Novella, Book 7.5)
Hellbound Warrior (Dark Warrior Alliance, Book 8)
Isobel (Dark Warrior Alliance, Book 9)
Rogue Warrior (Dark Warrior Alliance, Book 10)
Shattered Warrior (Dark Warrior Alliance, Book 11)
King of Khoth (Dark Warrior Alliance, Book 12)
Ice Warrior (Dark Warrior Alliance, Book 13)
Fire Warrior (Dark Warrior Alliance, Book 14)
Ramiel (Dark Warrior Alliance, Book 15)
Rivaled Warrior (Dark Warrior Alliance, Book 16)

Dragon Knight of Khoth (Dark Warrior Alliance, Book 17)
Ayil (Dark Warrior Alliance, Book 18)
Guild Master (Dark Alliance Book 19)
Maven Warrior (Dark Alliance Book 20)
Sentinel of Khoth (Dark Alliance Book 21)
Araton (Dark Warrior Alliance Book 22)
Cambion Lord (Dark Warrior Alliance Book 23)
Omega (Dark Warrior Alliance Book 24)
Dragon Lothario of Khoth (Dark Warrior Alliance Book 25)

Dark Warrior Alliance Boxsets:
Dark Warrior Alliance Boxset Books 1-4
Dark Warrior Alliance Boxset Books 5-8
Dark Warrior Alliance Boxset Books 9-12
Dark Warrior Alliance Boxset Books 13-16
Dark Warrior Alliance Boxset Books 17-20

Hollow Rock Shifters:
Captivity, Hollow Rock Shifters Book 1
Safe Haven, Hollow Rock Shifters Book 2
Alpha, Hollow Rock Shifters Book 3
Ravin, Hollow Rock Shifters Book 4
Impeached, Hollow Rock Shifters Book 5
Anarchy, Hollow Rock Shifters Book 6
Allies, Hollow Rock Shifters Book 7
Sovereignty, Hollow Rock Shifters Book 8

Midlife Witchery:
[Magical New Beginnings Book 1](#)
Mind Over Magical Matters
Magical Twist
My Magical Life to Live

Forged in Magical Fire
Like a Fine Magical Wine
Magical Yule Tidings
Magical Complications
Magical Delivery
Magical Moxie
In the Goddess's Magical Snare

Mystical Midlife in Maine
Magical Makeover
Laugh Lines & Lost Things
Hellmouths & Hot Flashes
Holiday with Hades
Saggy But Witty in Crescent City
Nasty Curses & Big Purses
Fae Forged Axes & Chin Waxes
Demonic Stones & Creaky Bones

Twisted Sisters' Midlife Maelstrom
Packing Serious Magical Mojo
Cadaver on Canal Street
Seances & Second Line Parades
French Quarter Fae

Bramble's Edge Academy:
Unearthing the Fae King
Masking the Fae King
Revealing the Fae King

Midnight Doms:
Her Vampire Bad Boy
Her Vampire Suspect
All Souls Night

OTHER WORKS BY BRENDA TRIM

Printed in Great Britain
by Amazon